THREE naughty NOVELLAS

IT TAKES TWO
ONE MORE RULE
TABLE FOR TWO

NIKKI SLOANE

Text copyright © 2017 by Nikki Sloane

Cover design © Shady Creek Designs

All rights reserved. Except as permitted under the U.S. Copyright Act of 1976, no part of this publication may be reproduced, distributed, or transmitted in any form or by any means, or stored in a database or retrieval system, without the prior written permission of the publisher.

The characters and events portrayed in this book are fictitious. Any similarity to real persons, living or dead, is coincidental and not intended by the author.

Audi Edition

ISBN 978-0-9983151-4-0

TABLE OF CONTENTS
and reading order

	PAGE
IT TAKES TWO	1
-THREE SIMPLE RULES-	
-THREE HARD LESSONS-	
ONE MORE RULE	67
-THREE LITTLE MISTAKES-	
-THREE DIRTY SECRETS-	
-THREE SWEET NOTHINGS-	
TABLE FOR TWO	189

IT takes TWO

THE BLINDFOLD CLUB PREQUEL

Chapter ONE

NINA

Music played from the speakers of my car, but cut off abruptly.

At least, I thought it did. It was hard to focus. The engine wasn't running now, because my keys were clenched in my fist, and I stared at the office building beyond my windshield.

The single story building was small and unassuming. Faded shingles wrapped along the roof, and the aluminum siding was worn. A few wayward weeds poked through the cracks in the broken sidewalk, but otherwise the place was in good shape. The sign on the glass doors had a logo and hours. The studio looked professional enough, much like any other office business. How many people knew what really went on behind those doors?

Deep breath. *You can do this.*

I tamped down the anxiety in my stomach and got out of my car. I had to lock it with the key because the car was twenty years old. Hell, the piece of shit was almost as old as me, but I shouldn't complain. It still ran, and it was free. Well, except for the bottle of coolant I had to put in it once a week. I couldn't afford to get the slow leak repaired. Thankfully, it had made the trip from Hammond, Indiana up to Chicago without an issue.

It was difficult to swallow my breaths as I teetered on my unaccustomed heels toward the studio. God, I needed a drink to calm my nerves. Even though I wanted this, it was still a huge step forward and one that couldn't be undone. The internet made things forever.

I placed a sweaty palm on the bar across the door and pushed it open.

The woman behind the desk glanced up. Her evaluating eyes peered directly into me, right past the blonde highlights I'd gotten last week, the spray tan, and the acrylic nails. I'd done all I could to make myself look the part.

Nina Hale, ready for stardom.

The office matched the outside. There was a large board with schedules written on it hanging on the back wall, and headshots pinned beside it. Computers, phones, fax machines. Everything was businesslike, even down to the desk clutter.

The skinny woman, who looked to be in her late forties, had brown hair with bangs, and just the right amount of makeup to look trashy-hot. Her red lips pulled back into a smile, but it was guarded.

"Are you Nina?"

I forced a warm, friendly smile. "Yeah."

"You don't look like your pictures."

Fuck. *Fuck!* We'd spoken on the phone, and she'd been clear that if I didn't match the pictures I submitted, they'd send me home immediately. "Uh, I changed my hair, but—"

The woman held up her hand, cutting me off. "You

look even better. You mind?" She spun her finger in the air, asking me to turn.

I tried not to wobble on the heels when I did as asked.

When I came back around, she was grinning. "Well, damn, girl. Aren't you something? I'm Kimberly."

I let out a relieved breath. "Nice to meet you." I bent over her desk and shook her outstretched hand.

Kimberly's gaze drifted beyond my shoulder, and then the door behind me creaked opened. I turned once more—

Oh my God.

The guy who stepped inside melted the panties I wore beneath my dress. He had that cocky frat boy look going on, a t-shirt stretched tight over his upper body, leaving nothing to the imagination. I could see how much this boy liked to work out. Jeans slung low on his hips and a baseball hat was turned backward, not shielding his gorgeous face.

He was the kind of guy who occasionally hit on me at the bars. I'd gone home with some of them, even let a few of them fuck me. But I'd learned they weren't interested in anything but pussy, and once they'd had it, it was time for them to move on.

This boy had an easy smile, which faded the edge of the cockiness just enough so I worried I might swoon like a fucking idiot. Was he the other talent? My heart lodged in my throat, clogging my ability to speak.

"Hey, Scott," Kimberly said.

"Hey," he echoed back. His gaze shifted my direction, starting at my feet and working up. He seemed to have no shame about the way he was drinking me in, and it made the nerves rattle harder in my belly.

"Scott, this is Nina," Kimberly said. "It's her first time."

Holy hell, his smile was amazing. It struck a balance between sweet and sinful, and his eyes lit up. "Yeah?"

I nodded because there was no telling what ridiculous sound I might make if I tried to speak.

"Nervous?" he asked.

I was. My knees were shaking under my dress, but I was determined not to show it. For months I had stared at the listing and fantasized about taking action, and once I had, more months passed as I completed all the steps necessary to bring me to today. No one knew where I was, except for the people in this room, and it fed into my fantasy. I could be *anyone* today.

I sucked in a calming breath. "I'm fine. Sort of excited."

He blinked, stunned. It was a reaction I was used to. I had a deep, smoky voice which didn't match people's expectations. They saw a pretty, feminine face with nice boobs and long legs, and assumed I'd have a high-pitched, girly voice to go along with it. It's not like I sounded like a man, but my alto voice caught people off guard.

"Excited?" His grin somehow widened. "I think we're gonna have a great time."

Kimberly rose from the desk. "Either of you want something to drink?"

My mouth was a desert from the realization I was going to be working with Scott. I'd assumed the guy would be decent looking, but not overly attractive. This guy looked delicious.

"Water?" I asked.

"Sure." Kimberly disappeared down the hall past a row of filing cabinets.

I could feel Scott's gaze on me like hands exploring my body, studying every curve, but I stared at the back wall. If everything went well, I'd see plenty of him in a few minutes.

The desk groaned softly as he leaned against it, and his shift in position wordlessly demanded my attention. So I turned my gaze to him and the dirty blond hair that curled at the ends beneath his baseball hat.

"What's a girl like you doing here?"

His gray-blue eyes were full of curiosity, not judgment. "I dunno," I said. "What's a *girl* like you doing here?"

His perfect mouth quirked into a half-smile at my barb. "I asked first, Nina. If that's your real name."

I'd gone back and forth, but in the end I decided to use my first name, not caring who knew. "It is my name, and I need the money." Not just that, I needed a whole new life.

"Yeah? Don't we all?" He rubbed a hand on the back of his neck, which gave an excellent view of his toned form. "Well, you're fucking hot. You'll have no problem getting lots of work."

It was a compliment, but he'd said it like it was fact. Coming from this sexy stranger, it was a huge turn-on. My face flushed with heat and I wavered slightly. "Thank you."

"Hey, if you get nervous . . . it's cool. Everyone is their first time."

So, he'd done this before. Relief passed through me. This was like dancing, and I was glad to have a strong partner to lead. "Were you?"

His expression was amused. "Yeah. I put a lot of pressure on myself and, fuck, I was awful. But don't worry." Scott flashed a devious grin. "I've gotten less awful since."

It was unstoppable that my gaze flowed down him. I couldn't imagine him being awful. No, something told me he'd be much, much better than *awful*.

Kimberly returned carrying two bottles of water. When she offered them to us, I took mine quickly, not wanting either of them to see my hand was shaking. Scott casually took the bottle, unscrewed the cap, and downed a long sip. He was cool as a cucumber.

"Well," Kimberly said, glancing up at the clock, "I guess we'll start without him. Either of you need a minute before we begin?"

"We're doing it without him?" Scott asked.

I wondered the same thing. Where was the director? We were going to shoot without one?

Kimberly shrugged. "Why not? Everyone else is here. No point wasting—"

The door flew open, and we all turned at the sound.

There was no way this guy was the director, he looked the same age as me. He had on flip-flops, cargo shorts and a polo shirt. Preppy, hot asshole, in the flesh.

Oh, good lord, who was this? I was annoyed at my body's response to him. He looked good, even though I didn't want him to. He pulled the aviator sunglasses down from his face, giving me a peek at his deep brown eyes. Wait a minute, was this who I was performing with? Kimberly hadn't said who, specifically, and neither had Scott. All he'd said was he thought we'd have a great time.

Both men were really attractive, and I'd only known Scott for two minutes, but in my flustered state, I'd cling to what I knew.

"You're running late," Kimberly said.

"I guess you didn't get my text. Sorry." The guy ran a hand through his almond-colored hair. "Traffic."

"Ben," she said, gesturing to us, "this is Nina and Scott. Scott does regular work for us, but she's new like you."

Ben's attention turned to me. I felt like a piece of meat under his heated scrutiny, but I also begrudgingly liked it. His appreciative stare was a needed confidence boost, like a pregame pep talk.

"You mind if we head straight back?" she said. He shook his head, his gaze never leaving mine. Good God, was the air conditioning working in this office?

"Okay, uh . . ." I said, unable to contain it. "I'm confused. Which guy am I with?"

"Shit, Kim." Scott's tone was annoyed. "You didn't tell her?"

Chapter TWO

Kimberly scowled. "She said she was up for multiples." She sighed and gave me her full attention. "It's both guys. Ben auditioned for us once before but he had an issue performing . . . I think having Scott there will help. But if it doesn't work out with Ben, we'll still have footage to use."

Oh. My. God.

"Jesus," Scott groaned. "You're gonna spring that on her thirty seconds before we get on set?"

She tried to hide her guilty expression and pushed her bangs out of her eyes. "You think it's a hardship to have two willing cocks?"

Everyone's eyes were on me, waiting to see my reaction. I didn't know it was possible to simultaneously be so thrilled and terrified. Both men. I was going to have both of these sexy guys at once.

"Girl, if you don't want to, that's no problem," she continued. "You can just pick one and we'll shoot a standard."

Both men hesitated. I didn't think either of them liked the idea of losing out, and how the fuck was I supposed to pick?

Ben's handsome face skewed with fleeting embarrassment. "There won't be any issues this time, I promise."

I'd never been with two at once, but holy hell, I'd fantasized about it. When I'd filled out the questionnaire for the studio on what I was willing to shoot, I'd gotten turned on just writing it down. But it sounded like more work to please two guys at once. "Does it pay extra?"

"It does, and you should know," her eyes gleamed mischievously, "two means twice the fun."

I pressed my knees together, containing the rush that moved through me. I wasn't going to live with regret at turning the opportunity down, and God knew I needed the money. "You don't have to sell me on it." My voice was tight, but strong. "I'm up for both."

Kimberly beamed. "I'd hoped you'd say that when you saw them."

Scott's face took a dark cast, like he wasn't pleased with Kimberly's manipulation.

My legs were jelly as I followed the group down the hall and through the doorway. Two diffused lights were suspended in each corner of the far wall, casting light into the room and on the main feature . . . the bed. It was king-size, made neatly with a white, fluffy comforter and a stack of pillows leaning against the headboard.

It was surreal to turn the corner from the office into a set that looked like a hotel bedroom, down to the nightstands with matching lamps. Well, except for the lighting and the sophisticated cameras on tripods. One on all three sides of the bed.

Kimberly went to a table in the back and picked up a handheld camera. "Nina, have a seat on the bed and get comfortable. I like to start with a short interview so both the guys and the viewers can get to know you better."

The bed was soft and I sank down into it, my gaze

fixed on her. It was becoming clear that the director wasn't late . . . she was already here. The feminist in me was both pleased that a woman stood at the helm of the studio, and also annoyed that I'd assumed the director would be male. Very little of this day had gone as I expected, and the camera wasn't even rolling yet.

The bed jostled as the guys sat on either side of me. Ben, on my right, sat a comfortable distance, but Scott was much closer. He leaned back casually on his arms, so one of his hands was behind me, his right leg up against my thigh. Not to be outdone, Ben slid closer. Every inch of my body was hyper aware of the two men who seemed to be circling before attack.

"When you get close," Scott said to Ben, "you let me know by putting your hand on her throat."

Ben's face clouded with unease. "You want me to choke her?" His gaze snapped my direction, silently demanding me to protest.

"No." Scott reached up, delicately setting his hand on the base of my neck. "Like this." My heart pounded at the contact of his warm fingers against my heated skin. There wasn't pressure in his touch. "Or if you're behind her, like this." His grip adjusted so his hand was wrapped around my throat, but his fingers simply rested there. Possessive and seductive.

Oh, man. Did he feel how hard I just swallowed? A smile teased his lips as his touch left me.

"We're not going to block the scene," Kimberly said. "Let's just have fun and do what everyone's feeling. I'll only speak up if it's needed." Her focus turned to me. "You're in good hands with Scott."

Her honest tone helped ease my nerves, and although she'd dropped the bomb of the threesome, I felt like my safety and comfort were more important than getting good footage.

There weren't any lights on the cameras signaling they were filming, but the air grew intense and serious when she stared down at the viewscreen. "Can you tell us your names?"

I wasn't sure who was supposed to speak, and exchanged a glance with Scott. "Ladies first."

I turned back to the camera. "I'm Nina."

As the guys introduced themselves, Scott took off his hat and tossed it aside, combing his fingers through his wavy hair. Was I subtly leaning toward him? I sat up straighter and turned to Ben, not wanting to show more interest in one over the other.

Ben had a strong jaw, a straight, Roman nose, and eyes like black holes. A force like gravity pulled me in. What would have happened if Ben had shown up first? Would I be leaning his direction?

We chatted for a while about how it was my first time, if I'd ever been with two guys at once, and I know I answered, but my brain raced a million miles an hour. Ben's fingertips skimmed along the bare skin of my thigh where the dress stopped, making me flinch. He chuckled at my reaction but held his hand up in surrender.

"Sorry," I said quickly. "You can touch me, you just

caught me by surprise."

He grinned and his fingers were back, tracing the edge of my dress. My breath stalled in my lungs when Scott swept the hair off of my shoulder and leaned in. Warm, damp lips settled on the nape of my neck and caused me to shudder.

My eyes hooded as both men touched me. Ben's hand slid along the length of my thigh while Scott's fingers pressed gently into my shoulder, holding me still. His mouth carved a path, his breath steaming across my skin, all while Kimberly and the cameras watched.

The air grew thick and heavy with lust.

My lips parted when I turned to Ben. His black eyes pinned me in place on the edge of the bed, while Scott continued to seduce me with his wicked mouth. I tilted my head to the side to give him more room, and he took it. *Fuck, he was good at that.* He used both tongue and teeth on the sensitive skin just beneath my ear.

A soft moan slipped from me, but both of the men must have heard it, because they acted like it was permission to go further. Ben eased my knees apart, and the pads of his fingers worked up, lifting my skirt with it. The thin fabric trailed and tickled softly as it went, all the way until my pale pink lace underwear was exposed.

Scott was inside the top of my dress, peeling the strap down with a firm hand. Every tiny centimeter of skin the men exposed brought me closer the point of no return, not that I cared anymore. Nina Hale, the girl who couldn't get anything better than an entry-level temp job, was about to go down in flames, and Nina the porn star would rise in her place.

The strap of my dress hung loose at my elbow and cool air wafted over my breast as Scott bared it for everyone to see. My nipples had tightened into hard peaks, aching for attention.

One of the guys made a sound of appreciation, but my lust-hazy mind couldn't determine which one. Ben's fingers tugged at the other strap, pulling the dress until it was a waded rope around my arms, holding me in place.

"Look at those perfect tits," Ben said. "You want me to suck on them?"

I didn't need to perform, my answer was genuine. "Yes."

"Not yet, Nina." Scott's voice was like the devil's. "We need to see all of you first."

Could the microphone pick up the way he said my name like it was dirty? And *special*? A rush of warmth spread between my legs.

"Show us," he commanded.

It was strange. I should have felt vulnerable, but the more undressed I became, the more power flooded through me. I pushed up to stand, no longer shaky on my heels, and shoved the dress down, stretching it over my hips until it was a puddle of fabric on the carpet.

"Goddamn, that is one fuckable ass," Ben said. His hand was warm on my cheek and squeezed, his rough fingers digging in. It felt good.

"I want to see that pussy, *Nina*," Scott said.

Kimberly had faded behind the lights. There were just the two men and the cameras now, but I was going to put on a show. I slipped my thumbs beneath the band at my hips and methodically worked the panties down, each side at a time to tease.

It was almost a growl in Scott's deep voice. "Get those panties off. Don't make us wait."

I shuddered with excitement and stepped out, until I was naked except for my glossy beige, open-toe high heels.

Ben stood up behind me, and his hands slid across my belly, one easing its way down to spread my pussy wide for the camera. The brush of his fingertips over my clit was electric. I bit down on my bottom lip, quieting my moan.

"Fuck, she's wet." His other hand curled around my breast, kneading it. I had to lean back against his chest for support, and clung to his strong forearm. Beneath his t-shirt, Ben's heart thumped along at a gallop. Was he nervous or turned on? I pressed further into him.

Oh. Definitely turned on.

"Oh my God," I said. His fingers stirred, one long stroke down and up, then circled where it felt best.

"You like that, don't you?" The voice just over my shoulder asked.

My lips pressed into a line and I nodded quickly, not wanting him to stop. Every nerve ending in me was alive and firing.

There was rustling as Scott climbed to his feet. His hand went over his shoulder, tugging a fistful of his shirt over his head until it was off and flung away. I inhaled sharply at the sight of his golden tan skin and the muscles rippling beneath it. My gaze followed the line of his body where his hips arrowed down into the sexy V, the best part just covered with the waistband of his boxers. It sat an inch above where his jeans stopped.

I was going to burst into flames.

Scott set his hand on my shoulder and urged me to turn into him, and then both men were touching me. My breasts, my ass, and the shortest strokes through my slit, torturing me. Ben's mouth found my earlobe and bit softly, but his hands were more aggressive. Sharp tugs of my nipples stole my breath.

The tremble in my legs was back.

It threatened to collapse me, and my palms flew forward, finding Scott's shoulders when he dipped down so he could wrap his lips around my breast. I stared at the top of his head with glazed eyes and hung on. Ben's support was gone so he could yank off his shirt, hurrying to keep up.

I could think of worse ways to make money than being sandwiched between two incredibly hot men while they were focused on me. I mean, I couldn't think of any worse ways right now, because my brain was functioning on only a basic level. The level that was all about need, and pleasure, and satisfaction.

They both radiated heat as they closed in. Hard chests were against me on both sides, flattening me between them. Scott's hand tangled in my hair and tugged my head back, forcing my gaze up to the ceiling, and the men descended on me like a pack feasting on their kill.

Chapter
THREE

I moaned as tongues traced the curve of my neck, and lips followed the line of my collarbone. All sense of what I was supposed to be doing was gone, and I allowed myself to be swept away in the sensations.

"Put your hands on our dicks," Scott whispered in my ear, quiet enough I was sure the microphone couldn't hear. My eyelids fluttered open and I blinked back into reality. Time to stop being so selfish.

"You gonna give me some hard cock?" I said, my tone forced. Shit, how lame did that just sound?

Ben didn't notice, or he covered for me. "You better fucking believe it."

Both men worked to undo their zippers as I reached to grasp them through their pants. It was awkward with my hand behind my back touching Ben, but holy shit. He was big. Scott was too, from what I could tell. I'd known I'd be working with a guy larger than average, but now a tiny part of me was freaking out. How was I going to handle *two* enormous cocks?

Anxiety climbed higher when Scott's jeans and boxers dropped, and I got my first look. It was a monster. His cock was long and thick, just like I'd expected from countless hours of watching porn, but that had been from behind the safety of my computer screen.

When I stood stunned and motionless, Scott grabbed

my hand and wrapped it tight around him, squeezing our hands closed. Then he began to fuck my fist. My mouth dropped open, watching him.

"That's so fucking hot," I gasped. His eyes flared with approval.

Ben's shorts were off, and I cupped my other hand around the fat head of his dick, stroking down the length.

"Oh, fuck, yeah." His hips pumped, spurring me on.

Scott's expression twisted with pleasure and Ben issued a loud sigh when I gripped them tighter. Damp, hard, and throbbing skin pushed against my palms, and the heavy breathing of the men was enough to make me ache. My pussy was dripping wet.

"On your knees, *Nina*."

I stared up into Scott's sky-blue eyes as I folded one leg beneath me, then the other, resting my knees on the carpet, my grip on the men never letting up. I'd seen enough porn to know what to do. I stroked my hands in sync, down their impressive lengths, and twisted as I came back up.

Without prompting, I swept my tongue over the tip of Scott's dick and he jerked under my hold. He stared down over his sculpted body to connect with mine, and the hunger in his eyes was dangerous and enticing. I parted my lips and took him in my welcoming mouth.

There was a sharp inhale from him through clenched teeth that sounded like a hiss, but was filled with satisfaction. Such a perfect sound, and it made me pause on Ben for a moment so I could hear it better.

"Don't fucking stop," Ben pleaded.

He moaned when I resumed my jerky hand job. The girls in the pornos made it look easy, but it wasn't. Concentrating on both men while also worrying about how I looked was exhausting. Plus it was insane what I was doing. Something so intimate, my first time with two men, who were strangers, all in front of another stranger and a camera. How wrong was it that I liked this?

No. There was something wrong with Nina the office temp. Nina the porn star had no shame.

I released Scott from my mouth and tore my gaze away from him, finding Ben's, which was fixed on me.

"So patiently waiting your turn," I said, my voice rasping.

His eyes turned an even darker shade of black and his expression was wild. Raw. Fuck, he looked good like that. His hand curled around the back of my neck and pulled me to him, slamming his cock in my mouth. There was so much force I had to let go of Scott and put both hands on Ben's hips to slow him down. Maybe he hadn't been so patiently waiting.

"Yeah, suck that cock," he whispered. In videos, I wasn't a fan of the dirty-talk. It felt fake and laughable, but here with Ben it was the opposite. I believed the words that tumbled from his lips. "Shit, that's good."

When I had Ben's pace under control, I reached back for Scott. Butterflies fluttered in my belly when his hand took mine and guided it, which made no sense whatsoever. I'd already sucked his dick. Why had an innocent touch caused this reaction?

Ben gathered my hair in his hands, keeping it out of my way and out of the shot, which was great. This was just as much his first role as it was mine. I looked up at him and wondered what had happened at his audition. There hadn't even been a hint of stage fright today.

He was in good shape. Not perfectly cut like Scott, but real. There was a different kind of sexiness in Ben's authenticity. I understood the hierarchy of our threesome. Scott was the top, the one controlling the scene, and I was all the way at the bottom, setting the rules. I was naturally submissive, so I had no issues with our roles. Was Ben comfortable in his?

My tongue swirled and cartwheeled on his cock, and it drew a shudder from him. It was sexy. His soft moans, coupled with the subtle tightening of his hold on my hair, showed me how much I was pleasing him. I felt powerful, even on my knees.

Scott's voice rang out from above. "I want her sucking your cock while I lick her pussy."

Oh, God, *yes*. Scott seized my arm and lifted me from my knees, pulling me off of Ben.

"Get up on the bed." It wasn't a request. The weight and authority in Scott's voice had my skin tingling, and me eager to obey.

He'd been talking to both of us. Ben climbed onto the bed, his naked body scurrying noisily over the sheets, and sat back against the headboard. His hard cock was clenched in a fist, pointing straight toward the ceiling.

Waiting for me.

There was fire and lust in his eyes as I stepped out of Scott's embrace and put a knee on the bed. I crawled as seductively as I could manage across the comforter, slowly making my way to Ben. The camera and Scott behind me, I assumed, could see every naked inch of my pussy, and I hoped it looked good.

"Fucking *shit*." Ben cursed on a long breath, one of his hands going to his forehead as I ran the edge of my tongue from base to tip of his heated, damp flesh. Then I swirled over the slit and the parted legs around me quivered.

The bed jostled as Scott joined us. His hand caressed the round curve of my ass, which was up in the air. I buried my knees and elbows into the mattress, flipped my hair over a shoulder, and wrapped my lips around Ben's dick. Scott's fingers skimmed through my pussy, feathering the softest touch.

I whimpered and bobbed faster on Ben, like pleasing him would somehow earn me a reward from Scott, which I was desperate for. I needed him to touch me. I wanted him to taste me. Oh, God, *please* . . .

Wet velvet teased at my seam, parting me. Fuck, that tongue was going to turn me into liquid. I hollowed out my cheeks, sucking hard on the cock in my mouth, and my moan mingled to match Ben's.

Scott's tongue was ruthless, fucking me out of my mind. I shifted my hips back against his face, the stubble of his whiskers gritting against the inside of my thighs. A storm of electricity swirled low in my belly, its static slashing upward as my orgasm gathered strength.

Holy shit.

I had to pause to catch my breath, pulling Ben from my mouth as a finger sank inside me. Deep inside, stretching me. I moaned with his cock against my lips, "Yes."

It was hard to concentrate when all I wanted to do was enjoy. Scott's deliberate tempo and indecent tongue rattled every thought away, except for the one repeating: *come*. Over and over. I panted, one hand gripping Ben's inner thigh and the other slowly stroking his cock, trying to stay on task.

"She really seems to like that," Ben said, throwing his smug words over my head toward the man making me insane. I moaned, loud and long, in case they needed further proof. My nails dug into Ben's skin as the orgasm closed in around me, making me search for something to hold on to.

Scott's tongue fluttered on my clit, his finger driving hard and fast, hitting just the right spot.

"Shit," I cried. "Oh my God. I'm gonna . . . I'm coming!"

Pleasure detonated inside and burst through my muscles, sending a wave of ecstasy that was so powerful I couldn't breathe. My body seized and locked up, pulsing on the finger that remained inside. A final swipe of his tongue made me flinch, the pleasure so intense it was acute and verging on pain.

Ben's fingers skimmed my forehead, brushing my hair out of my eyes so he could gaze at me while I struggled to recover. "Did you like coming all over his face, while sucking my hard cock?"

I nodded and shuddered with an aftershock, lost in his eyes that were as pitch-black as night. I held his stare while my shaky lips parted, slowly descending around him. The blood that rushed loudly through my ears began to slow and I matched its languid pace, fucking Ben with my mouth.

Scott's lightly calloused palm closed on my hip, gently urging me to turn. His voice was soft and surprisingly sweet. "On your back, Nina."

The juxtaposition of Ben's dirty words against Scott's careful ones couldn't have been more perfect. It kept the fire burning in me even after my need for satisfaction had ebbed, hinting at a new swell on the horizon.

I rolled over until the sheets were cool against the flushed, heated skin of my back, and Ben moved, tucking his knees beneath him so both men towered over me. Being caught under their gazes was a web ensnaring my body, a power I was more than willing to submit to. Scott stood at the edge of the bed. He hooked his hands under my knees and slowly slid me across the mattress toward him, spreading my legs.

I swallowed a breath.

We wouldn't be using condoms for the scene. All actors had to be screened and tested twice before committing to the shoot, and I'd had to prove I was using birth control. It was as safe as the situation could be, but it didn't feel any less dangerous when Scott ran the length of his bare cock against my wet pussy.

Every muscle in me tensed. Ben was in my hand, his

cock growing hard as steel when Scott gripped himself and positioned the tip at my entrance, readying to take me.

The man between my legs held an expression painted with desire, and he focused first on my eyes before sweeping his gaze down along my nude flesh, all the way to the tiny space separating us.

"Watch," Scott said.

Holy.

Fuck.

Chapter FOUR

The head of Scott's cock disappeared as he slowly buried himself inside me, an uncomfortable and yet pleasurable stretch that went on forever. I gasped and arched my back, trying to watch, but the sensation was too much. Too full. Too good.

When he was fully seated inside, he gave me a moment to adjust. Ben's fingers danced over my breast, tweaking a nipple, while his other hand urged me to stroke him faster. His attention seemed acutely tuned to what Scott was doing, and . . . was there a tiny flare of envy in his dark eyes?

"Oh my God." I started to writhe as Scott moved his hips, grinding himself against my swollen clit. "Fuck me," I whined. "Please, fuck me now."

The smile that flashed across Scott's lips was wicked victory, and he awarded me with his first thrust. A moan tore from my throat. Pinpricks of bliss tingled at the base of my spine as he found his rhythm, a mind-numbing pace to drive into me and rock the bed.

"Yeah, girl," Ben said. "Fucking take that cock."

I wasn't sure which he meant, because he crept closer on his knees until he was against my shoulder, setting his cock on my lips. It didn't matter, I was enjoying both men. The vibrations from Scott's thrusts reverberated up my body, and I opened my mouth, sliding my lips along Ben's thick, veiny shaft.

Were the cameras able to capture a fraction of how erotic this was? Did I look good with one man between my legs, fucking me while my tits bounced and my tongue wrapped around the cock of another man? Both of them had their hands on me then, one on each breast, massaging and pinching.

My moans built in urgency. Scott's hips slammed against mine, and my fingers shot down to rub my clit, deepening my pleasure. A bead of sweat trickled down from his temple. It was hot under the lights, and hotter still from how he was fucking me. Hard, and deep. His chest heaved, and the air was punctuated by his gasps for breath, a byproduct of the intense physical exertion. The slide of him into my body, then out right to the edge, and plunging back in . . . it repeated endlessly.

His hands clasped tightly around my thighs, lifting me into each of his punishing thrusts. The force of it rammed my back into the mattress. Could he feel how badly he made my legs shake? God, watching him cranked up my own desire, and I wanted this to go on forever.

But it couldn't.

There were two men, and no matter how I tried, I was sure my mouth and hand weren't enough to satisfy my other partner.

I stared up at Ben, squeezing my hand like a vise around him. "You want to fuck this pussy?"

Scott pulled out and flung a finger at the bed, his gaze on Ben. "Lay down so she can ride you."

It took Ben no time to comply. His head hit the

pillows and he stroked himself, waiting for me expectantly while Scott helped me to my feet. But Scott's arms locked around me, smashing my body to his at the same moment his lips crashed against mine in a kiss.

Whoa.

My head spun, totally unprepared for it. Kissing right in the middle of the scene? And *only* kissing? He gripped my ass while his tongue filled my mouth, claiming every inch, like he was possessing me. And the strangest thing of all about the impromptu kiss was the passion behind it. It felt . . . honest. Needy.

My eyes had to be impossibly wide as Scott drew away from my lips, one hand cradling my jaw, and his thumb brushed tenderly over my cheekbone. Well, there were my weak knees again. The corner of his mouth lifted in a disarming smile.

"You okay?" he whispered.

"Yeah." My voice wavered, though. I wasn't sure how to vocalize what I needed. "Can I have . . . more?"

Surprise washed over his handsome face, and the corner of his mouth twitched. He forced me to turn in his arms, pulling me back against his sweat-dampened chest, and there was nowhere else to look but at the man lying prone on the bed, waiting for me.

Scott whispered against the shell of my ear. "If it gets to be too much, tell me to make you come and I'll know you want to stop."

He released his hold at the same moment Ben offered a hand to me. Scott's words echoed in my mind as

I climbed on the bed. His concern over the next part of the scene, his genuine kiss . . . did he know what he was doing to me?

Ben grinned as I took his hand and climbed into his lap, positioning myself over him. He braced my hips and gently urged me down, his cock intruding.

"Oh, fuck yes." The muscles along his jaw flexed like he was clenching his teeth. "Get that pussy on me."

I gasped when he pulled down and impaled me on his hard dick. He didn't give me time to catch my breath. The hands rocked my hips, guiding me to ride. I sat upright, palmed my breast, and then began to fuck him.

This was more of what I had expected. A show, although it felt far better than I'd thought it would. When his hand crushed my other breast, I arched my back and moaned, embellishing the performance.

"Yeah, so fucking good," he moaned. Ben's mouth was open, and he sucked in air while his black eyes seemed to study me, evaluating every reaction I made to his movements. His legs were spread and feet flat against the mattress so he could thrust up into me like a piston.

I rode him like that for a while, until I was panting and needed to adjust. So I leaned forward, putting my palms flat on Ben's chest for leverage, and his legs relaxed, giving me room to work.

But a hand came down against my ass, causing me to jolt. It hadn't hurt, but the surprise of it made me pause and turn to Scott, a tiny yelp falling from my lips. He'd vanished from the scene when I'd gotten on top, but now he sat beside us on the bed. His palm remained against my cheek and the burn lingered, but he rubbed it softly.

"You're right," he said to the other man. "She does have a fuckable ass."

Scott's fingers skated over my skin, dipping down between my cheeks, and even though I'd implied it, my heart lurched into my chest. There was a clear squeeze bottle in his other hand. Lube.

The pads of his fingers probed as he seemed to gauge my comfort level with anal. The orgasms it gave me were epic, but . . . I'd never had full double-penetration. I was excited, and nervous, but I had a way out if I needed it. This had been what Scott meant when he'd whispered in my ear.

Ben's cock was throbbing inside me and I continued to squirm on it while Scott moved to kneel behind us. His fingers lifted my cheek to the side, and cold liquid dripped down, gliding through my crevice.

There was a thump as the bottle fell to the bed, and the fingers of both of Scott's strong hands fanned out on my ass, then curled, digging in. He urged me to ride faster, which I did. I gripped at Ben's sweaty chest as I kept up the fast pace, and one of Scott's hands began to move, creeping inward. Two fingers glided to my center and pressed firmly on my other entrance.

"Oh," I cried when he gained access. It was shocking and dirty, and my eyes wanted to roll back into my head from how good it felt. Ben wrapped his hands on my biceps, bracing me.

"You look like you need another cock inside you." God, Ben's mouth turned me on. The muscles inside my pussy clenched on him and I watched his pupils dilate in reaction. His face had a faint sheen of sweat and lust.

"Yes," I moaned, barely intelligible. It was indecent fucking one man while another possessed me this way, and it felt better than anything ever.

Scott's other hand went to my shoulder, and the fingers in my ass retreated. Seconds later, the tip of his cock was right there. He squeezed his hold, fingers brushing my jaw, and I looked over my shoulder at him, filled with anxiety.

The lights cast a glow around him, but I could see well enough. He looked fucking gorgeous, but his expression was serious. "Deep breath and don't move."

Beneath me, Ben went rigid. Scott's hand on my shoulder coursed down over my trembling back, following the line of my spine, until it moved to settle on a hip. He seemed to be waiting for something.

I filled my lungs with air, and only then did he start to press into me.

"Oh, oh, oh . . ." Oh my God! It was a burning, stretching sensation—one I wasn't entirely sure I liked. I felt overwhelmed. Full beyond reason. Scott's gaze never left mine as he pushed deeper into my ass. I was sure he was expecting any second for me to tell him to make me come.

"Jesus," Ben groaned. Even without movement, he seemed to be enjoying it. His fingers bit into my arms, distracting me from my discomfort. Fuck, Scott's cock was huge. My body was shuddering violently, but—

"Fuck." I spat it out, unable to find any other word, because Scott began to move, and sensations shifted. Displeasure turned on its side and tumbled into enjoyment.

My curse word was a starting pistol on the men. Scott's hands clamped on my waist and he withdrew, only to sink back into me. The fiery body beneath me stretched up, pushing inside with slow, shallow strokes.

"Yes," I cried.

Scott moved a little faster, a little deeper, finding a tempo. He lifted his foot and placed it flat on the mattress to give him a better stance.

"Yes, yes, yes . . ." I chanted it, speeding my rhythm as Scott did his.

"It's so fucking tight." Ben's eyes slammed shut and his mouth rounded as he exhaled loudly. "Oh, fuck."

I'd never felt so dominated. These men using my body simultaneously for their pleasure, but also mine . . . I fucking loved it. My moans built in a crescendo until they bordered on screams, but I'd lost all control. I hovered right at the edge as Ben's body rubbed my clit, filled my pussy, and Scott fucked my ass, sending my nerves into overdrive.

An inferno of need and heat smothered me, and my fingers clawed at the sheets, gripping them furiously. Scott's hands clamped on my waist and clenched so hard it was at the edge of pain, but his movement held the same effect his tongue had given me earlier. Only one thought, one need in my mind.

Come, come, come . . .

That was when the orgasm took me. My heart stopped, my breath stuck in my lungs, and for a moment, I couldn't vocalize how good it felt. My ability to do anything was obliterated.

A final thrust from Scott restarted me, and I screamed in ecstasy. The shattering, falling-apart sensation stormed through my bloodstream, and bliss thundered behind it, wiping everything out.

I collapsed forward, burying my face into the side of Ben's neck, breathing him in. He smelled faintly of pine, and sweat, and sex. Both men continued to drive into my spent body, only the muscles beneath me were tense. Ben's hand lay gently around my throat. His signal that he was close.

Scott jerked me, pitching me to the right, flinging me on my back. He loomed above, stroking himself furiously and the thick muscle of his arm flexed as he pumped. It was quite the view.

Ben scrambled onto his knees beside me, jerking himself, angling his cock at my tits. He only lasted a few seconds before he gasped, and his hand slowed.

"Here it fucking comes."

Ribbon after ribbon struck me, thick and hot. His long moans filled the set, and I watched, mesmerized. Seeing someone else come was erotic and fascinating. His hand clutched tight and he sat back on his heels, almost as if admiring his work.

My gaze naturally went to the other man who was

still pumping. I lifted up on my elbows to watch better. Should I touch him? Would he let me?

No. Tension pinched Scott's shoulders together and his back bowed. His breath left him in a sharp burst as his freehand curl into a fist. His cum shot out in spurts, flicking onto my belly, wave after warm wave.

He slowed to a stop and he threw himself forward, planting his hands on the mattress on either side of my head. He lowered down so his lips were a breath away. He'd brought himself ninety-five percent of the way, it was up to me to do the rest.

So I reached up behind his head, clenched a fistful of hair, and drew him down into my kiss. Time came to a halt when his mouth was on mine. His tongue slipped past my lips, sliding over mine as if savoring my taste.

I was vaguely aware when Ben took my hand in his and laced our fingers together. It was an intimate gesture, made more so when he lifted our joined hands and kissed the back of my palm.

It was quiet and peaceful.

"Wow," a female voice said. "That was fabulous, you guys."

Chapter
FIVE

Scott straightened back from me, his expression pleased. Was it from Kimberly's comment, or that I had kissed him? I wanted it to be the latter.

"Whenever you're ready," she continued, "I'll have your checks at my desk. Bathroom's right through the door to the left."

She went. The overhead set lights clicked off and faded to dark, leaving the room only lit by the lamps on the end table. It made everything feel real and . . . oh, God. I was sticky, and what the fuck had I just done?

It was like Scott could sense the panic rising in me. He stood swiftly from the bed, and heavy footsteps carried him away. A faucet ran, sounds of hands being washed came from the next room, and I turned my blank stare to Ben. He was sitting up, still clasping my hand. His thumb brushed back and forth in a comforting gesture.

"You did awesome," he said. "I was so nervous."

"You were?" I blinked. "I couldn't tell."

Scott reappeared, holding a damp washcloth, and he approached the bed.

"That's cold!" I cried as he began to rub it on me.

"Sorry." But he continued to wipe the wet terrycloth against my skin, cleaning the evidence of what we'd done. Yet another unexpected gesture from him. Wasn't he supposed to bolt now that we'd finished?

THREE *naughty* NOVELLAS

The bed shifted when Ben climbed off. He padded into the bathroom and shut the door, leaving Scott and me alone. I felt more vulnerable now with him, which was fucking ridiculous. He set the washcloth beside me on the bed as I sat up, and his expression changed to one that looked . . . odd. The confident, professional porn star appeared off-balance.

"Kimberly should have told you."

I shrugged, unsure what to say or how to feel. "I had a great time."

"Good. That's . . . good."

Was he nervous? He combed a hand through his hair, and when it came down, it fell to rest comfortably on my thigh. I stared at him, puzzled. His palm against my skin felt nice, but also confusing. There weren't cameras to perform for. Was Scott . . . was he *into* me?

"Nina."

My name in his voice wasn't playing fair. The room was suffocating and hot under his intense stare. I wanted to melt into him, but at that second the bathroom door swung open, breaking the spell of the moment. Ben strolled to his clothes and began to get dressed.

"Seriously, guys," he said, tugging a leg into his cargo shorts. "You both were great. I'd love to work with either one of you again."

"Yeah." Scott broke my gaze and went to my wad of clothes. "Same here." By the time I was standing, he was beside me, dropped my dress in my hands, and urged me toward the bathroom.

Behind the closed door, I cleaned up quickly and tried to assemble my thoughts, but also didn't want to waste time. Curiosity about Scott ate at me. I needed to catch him before he left because I wasn't ready for my time with him to be over.

I blew out a quiet sigh of relief when I spotted him standing by Kimberly's desk. It looked like Ben had already gone, but Scott lingered, chitchatting with her.

"Your check," she said, thrusting the paper at me. "You better believe you'll be hearing from me again. You two were on fire."

I took the check and risked a glance at Scott. His expression was unreadable, but it made my heart race all the same.

"Don't worry," she added, looking up at him with a teasing smile. "I won't tell Kendall about the kissing." She winked at me. "Kendall's his girlfriend."

My blood turned to slush in my veins, and I couldn't stop the accusing tone. "You have a girlfriend?"

He glared at Kimberly. "No. We broke up two months ago."

Her face filled with shock, and then she had what looked like an epiphany. "You know, I wondered why you guys weren't doing as many scenes together." She shrugged, an 'oh, well.'

"Can I walk you out?" he asked.

Oh, good lord. Weak knees and high heels were a terrible combination, and my car was a long way across the parking lot. Five whole spots. How the hell was I going to make it? I nodded slowly.

It was still warm, even though the sun was setting. My shoes clip-clopped on the broken pavement as I pointed out my piece-of-shit car. I'd spent so much of the day being nervous I no longer had a filter.

"You shot porn with your girlfriend?"

"Ex-girlfriend, but yeah, sometimes. Sometimes with other people."

I couldn't wrap my head around it. "She didn't mind you sticking your dick in other women?"

"Not really. It didn't bother me when she worked with other guys. I'm not the jealous type, and it's acting."

"Oh." He probably had no idea, but his comment stung. I'd foolishly thought there'd been more than just acting between us.

When we reached my car, he stopped and put his hands on his hips, facing me. "Sex on screen with other people is okay. It's just about money and getting off. But kissing someone else . . . that's different."

Kimberly's teasing replayed in my mind. Kissing meant something to Scott. A connection possibly more intimate than sex. "You kissed me."

A slow smile dawned on his lips. "Yeah. More than once."

Butterflies and jelly knees. God, was I a teenager?

He closed the distance between us, setting one hand in the small of my back and the other on my cheek. "I'm going to kiss you again, and then you're going to come home with me."

I was thrilled, but I tried to play it cool. "That's presumptuous."

"It's a fact, *Nina*."

I shivered. "Oh, really?"

"Really. There's an enormous puddle of coolant under this car. It's not going anywhere."

"Oh, no." I glanced down and a puddle of purple-green fluid reflecting back at me. Scott was absolutely right. My bottle of coolant in the backseat was almost empty—there was no way I'd make it back home.

I opened my mouth to say something, although I wasn't sure what, but he cut me off. His lips sealed over mine, kissing me with complete abandon. I balled my fists into his shirt, greedy for the contact. It did feel far more intimate than anything else we'd done.

He took my hand in his and tugged me toward his pickup truck on the opposite side of the lot. "This works out better all around," he said.

"How exactly does my POS car needing a new radiator work out better?" I muttered.

He unlocked his truck and pulled open the passenger door for me. "I have a friend who just opened a new club, and I know he'd love to meet you. How do you feel about being tied up or blindfolded during sex?"

My brain stumbled over his question. "It's . . . fine, I guess. I haven't really done it."

"You haven't?" His tone was pleasantly surprised. "The girls at Joseph's club make a ton of money. Triple that check in your purse."

I froze. "Triple a week?"

"A night."

Nina the office temp died from shock. "Scott, I need a favor."

He gazed at me as if reading my thoughts. "You want me to blindfold you and tie you up, and see if you're into it?" He laughed at my serious expression. "Oh, you will be, but don't worry. We can do it anyway, just to be sure."

I grinned and got into his truck.

Chapter SIX

SCOTT

I'd been blessed with an eight-inch dick and a good-looking face. I lived in the gym. I had stamina, a rock-hard erection, and enough respect for my career to research the shit out of it. I'd try any tip I stumbled across on a porn blog, always did my best to maintain good relationships with my castmates and crew, and networked like hell.

In porn, women were the stars.

But I was going to make the name Scott Westwood known.

Things were changing in the industry all the time. Emphasis was on producing *real* now. No cheesy music, bad sets, and ridiculous plots. No canned lines of dirty talk. The high def cameras demanded 'honest' acting. The viewer wanted to feel the attraction and connection between performers, along with believable orgasms.

As a dude, it was ultra-competitive, but I could handle the pressure. I always performed, and made sure both my partners and the cameras were satisfied, even if there wasn't attraction. Shit with Kendall had been messy, but none of it showed when we worked together post-breakup.

There was absolutely no issue with attraction this afternoon when I'd first seen Nina. I glanced over at her now as we waited at a stoplight. She flashed a nervous smile.

She might have been the most beautiful girl I'd ever seen, and that was before her clothes came off.

Shit, just thinking about it made me sweat. I reached over and turned up the air conditioner fan speed, then wrapped my fingers around the gear shift. I was still buzzing from her kiss, riding a contact high.

Kissing her during the shoot had probably shocked me more than her. I hadn't planned to do it. As soon as my lips touched hers, I was done for. Gone.

"He didn't kiss you," I said abruptly, the heat of her making it hard to think.

"Ben?" She laced her fingers together in her lap, like she wasn't sure what to do with her hands. "No." She took in a breath, and her voice went soft, as if shy. "I'm glad he didn't."

A smile twitched on my lips. "Me, too."

While I didn't get jealous when it came to sex, kissing her... I was grateful not to have to share that with him. I'd known the shoot would have another guy on set, with the potential of a multiple scene, but then Ben had been late.

"I thought," I said, "he wasn't going to show, and I was going to get you all to myself." The disappointment had been strong when he'd arrived.

Her breathing picked up. "All to yourself. Don't you have that now?"

My smile grew. She'd made it pretty clear there was no contest which man she preferred, and it turned me on. Deep down, every guy was competitive. Knowing she chose me was a huge ego boost.

"Yeah," I said, grinning.

I could hardly wait. I hadn't fucked anyone without a camera watching in months. Spending time with Nina, who I was genuinely interested in, was exciting. We clicked on a sexual level, and I was anxious to see if we matched in other places, too. Worst case scenario, we'd have some more great sex and then go our separate ways. Best case scenario? Who knew? We had chemistry. She was obviously cool with my job, and I was with hers, so there was potential for . . . more. Maybe some kind of a future.

Okay, calm down. It was way too soon to be thinking about that.

"I love this song," she said. She leaned over and turned the radio up, drowning out conversation. Of course it was my current favorite rap song, the one I'd listened to endlessly on repeat and knew every word.

She did, too.

The sun was setting and it cast warm light on her sexy face. Thank fuck it wasn't a long drive to my place on the south suburbs of Chicago. I was already thinking of all the ways I wanted to have her, completely to myself, with no one directing how it was supposed to go down.

She'd made the sexiest noises in that deep, throaty voice of hers. Blood flowed south of my belt, pumping into my dick. I tightened my grip on the steering wheel as she mouthed the words, keeping up with the fast tempo. As soon as the song faded out, I turned the dial down so she could hear me.

"I have to tell you, Nina," I said. "That was the hottest

scene I've ever done."

She halted as if stunned by my words.

And then, she came to life. Her face burst into a smile and she set her hand on my thigh, squeezing. "The way you say my name, it's so sexy."

I wished I drove an automatic for the first time in my life, only so I could put my hand on top of hers and drag it exactly where I wanted it, but rush hour traffic made it impossible, and it'd be dangerous anyway.

How had I gotten so impatient? I'd learned some tricks to back myself off the edge of orgasm, to not give in to what I wanted. Shit, was I going to have to use those skills now? *Pleasure will come*, I promised myself. *Just not right this moment.*

We barely said a word the rest of the drive since the sexual energy between us was taut. My skin was itchy as we got off the freeway and headed toward my house. I had a blindfold somewhere in my place; it had been included in a travel kit when I'd gone overseas for a photo shoot. Where had I put it? The bottom drawer of my dresser?

I could improvise if I couldn't find it. Same with the restraints. I hadn't been to Joseph's blindfold club, but I understood the setup. I had some rope in the garage left over from landscaping that would work, assuming Nina was game.

I turned into the driveway and hit the remote. Nina's eyes widened as she took in my place. It wasn't big or impressive-looking, but the two-bedroom bungalow was all mine. We slid into the shade of the garage, I parked, and shut off the engine.

Her hand drew away from my leg, but otherwise there was no movement. She didn't reach for the door handle.

"Didn't think you'd end up here?" I said.

"No," she admitted. "I wasn't sure I'd even shoot the scene."

"You were that nervous?"

"No." Her blonde hair shimmered as she shook her head. "I didn't know if I was going to get the greenlight."

"Are you kidding? You're so fucking hot."

She stared at me with big eyes filled with disbelief, so I could tell she wasn't fishing for a compliment. What was it with women? I'd met a few who were overconfident about their looks, but generally girls had self-esteem issues. Lots of pretty women were walking around believing they were less attractive than they were. I liked a humble person more than a cocky one, but confidence? It was fucking sexy.

Pink flashed over her cheekbones at my compliment. "Thanks."

"Come on," I said. "Let's go inside and figure out what to do about your car."

What I really wanted to do was to put my mouth on hers again. The drug of Nina was beginning to fade and I was desperate for another hit. I shoved my door open and hurried around the front of the truck while she reached for her purse, which allowed me to open the passenger door for her.

Just because I shot porn, sometimes even the rough

stuff, didn't mean I wasn't a gentleman in real life. From the minute I'd been introduced to her, I was hell-bent on making Nina feel comfortable. Coming home with a guy she'd just met, even though we'd acted together, had her guard up, and I lived alone. She had a right to be cautious.

I let her into my kitchen first, and then hurried around her, wishing I could block the view. The place was a disaster. "Uh, yeah. The dishes kind of got away from me."

She smiled as I guided her on into the living room.

Also a disaster.

I grabbed the open pizza box off the coffee table and folded it up, tossing it into the kitchen. "Gimme a second to—"

"Seriously, Scott, don't worry about it." Amusement played on her expression. Her gaze roamed over the couch littered with two PS4 controllers and the end table covered in empty Mt. Dew cans.

I owned my house, but I felt nothing like an adult now, and I didn't want Nina to see me as a boy. My messiness hadn't bothered Kendall because she was a bigger slob than me, but I could be better than this.

"I've got an idea," I said. "I'll call my friend who works at a garage while you hop in the shower." I rubbed my palm on the back of my neck, and then offered my hand out. "I mean, if you want a shower."

She paused. "I do, but . . ."

"It's not gross in there, I swear." Oh shit, was it? I tried to recall the state of my bathroom this morning. Nothing stood out, but I'd have to get in there first just to be safe.

"No." She laughed lightly. "I mean, it seems weird using your shower when we just met."

I blinked. The longer we went without touching, the further she slipped into shyness. Where was the girl who'd asked me for *more* during our scene? I reached for her, trapping her small waist in my hands and tipped my face down to hers. "You let me fuck you, Nina." I emphasized her name the way she seemed to like it, and slid a hand down until it cupped a handful of her ass. "I had my dick *here*. The least I can offer you is the use of my shower."

I bent the last inch and set my lips on top of hers, igniting our kiss. Instantly her mouth was open, accepting my tongue as I sought out hers. It was electric. The buzz roared back to full strength when my tongue swept in her mouth, and she pressed her lips against mine, answering with the same intensity.

When it ended, she swayed under my hands. Warmth spread across my chest at my effect on her.

"Okay." Her voice was as unsteady as her body. "I'll use your bathroom which you say is not gross."

I nodded enthusiastically. "That's *probably* not gross."

For fuck's sake, it was.

I grabbed my damp towel off the floor where I'd left it and used it to scrub the counter clean as quickly as possible. At least the shower tub was okay. I tossed my dirty towel into the hallway and grabbed a new one down from the shelf in the closet. It was a beach towel, but whatever. It was clean.

"Are you, uh, joining me?" Her eyes seemed to spark

with excitement at the idea.

"If you don't mind, sure." But then I thought about what I still needed to do. "Get started without me, I'll make the call and be back in a few minutes."

Nothing would kill the mood faster than her seeing my underwear and socks covering the bedroom floor.

I called my friend, explained the situation, and he offered to drive over to the studio and check her car out on his way to work tonight. When I had everything shoved in the closet and the bed made, I found the blindfold and rope, tucked them under a pillow, and headed for the shower.

The curtain was drawn so I couldn't see her, and I wasn't sure if she'd heard the door open and close. I didn't want to startle her. "Ready for company?"

She laughed softly. "As long as that company doesn't get my hair or face wet. I don't want to redo my makeup and I'm sure you don't have a hair dryer."

"No, I don't." I pulled back the curtain, revealing a nude and glistening Nina. "Fuck me running," I groaned as I stepped into the tub. "Kimberly needs to put you in a shower scene."

Nina moved out of the way, making room for me to get under the angled stream of water, but her gaze swept down my frame and lingered appreciatively on my dick.

Which was already growing hard for her.

"Do you always work for Kimberly?"

"No, I've worked with some others. The pay's better at Wicked Entertainment, but they run things differently. It's not really my style. Kim's is more laid back, and I have more fun there."

I scrubbed my hands through my hair under the shower, grabbed my all-in-one shampoo, and worked up a lather, trying to hurry along. The water did nothing to dampen my appetite.

"How long have you been doing it?"

I paused while I thought. "Three years?" I resumed my washing, surprised it had been that long. Sometimes I still felt new. "I didn't start getting regular work until last year."

"You like it?"

"Getting paid to fuck? Hell yeah." Occasionally, I got to be with two women at once, and they paid *me* for that. "Sometimes it's work, but for the most part, it's a pretty sweet deal."

She hesitated, and then blurted the question out. "Is that how you met you last girlfriend?"

No, I definitely hadn't met Kendall on set. "We were a couple before. We did an amateur casting couch thing." I fought to keep the embarrassment from my voice. "Remember when I said I was awful my first time? It was with her."

I rinsed the last of the shampoo from my hair, running my hands over my chest and lower, cleaning off. Nina's gaze followed the path of my hands and I swallowed hard. If I stroked myself, would she take over? I was ready to find out.

"Can I ask what happened with you two?"

I froze mid-stroke and abandoned my grip. "Yeah,

sure. Having sex in front of the camera can be addicting. We got to a point where she didn't want to fuck me unless someone else was watching."

Nina's mouth dropped open and shock blanketed her face. "Oh, that's ridiculous."

I chuckled. "Yeah, I thought so, too. The breakup was mutual."

She drew in a deep breath, but yet her voice was rushed, like she wanted to say it before she ran out of courage. "I'm happy to fuck you when no one's watching."

She crossed her arms over her chest and shivered, probably because I was hogging all the water. I stepped to the side, ignoring how the shower curtain clung to me.

"Come here," I whispered. She hadn't a clue how badly I needed to hear that, and I was more than ready to show her some appreciation.

Chapter SEVEN

Nina took a tentative step forward, and it was all the opening I needed. I wrapped my arms around her and slammed my mouth over hers, letting our slick bodies press against each other.

My cock grew so hard it was painful, and the ache intensified when she ran her fingers down my length. We groped and explored, sliding our wet hands over smooth skin.

God, it was so fucking nice to enjoy. There weren't thoughts about lighting, or my bicep blocking a camera angle, or any of that. My focus was only on her, and me, and *us*. Her touch began hesitant but grew confident, and she gripped me firmly, making my heartbeat climb.

"I'm getting ready to take away your hands," I mumbled against her mouth, "so enjoy it while you can."

I could have been talking to myself.

Like everything else, her kiss started as a slow burn and escalated until it was wildfire. We mashed our mouths together, panting and nipping, hungry for more. I brushed my palm over her perfect tits as I worked my way down the curve of her body.

I eased one finger inside her, followed instantly by a second one, where it was scorching hot.

She moaned it in her smoky voice. "*Fuck.*"

The word shot down my spine, and arrowed into my

groin like a knife of desire. Nina had both arms wrapped around my shoulders, but she reached a hand up, maybe looking for something else to cling to. She gripped the shower curtain and bucked in my hold as I fucked her, driving my fingers deep inside.

She gasped for breath, and suddenly the plastic curtain began to rip, tearing free of the rings.

"Oh, shit!" she cried.

We both froze and stared at the damage. The cheap curtain sagged in the middle, barely hanging on to the rod. She looked horrified, but a laugh bubbled up deep inside me.

"You better get in my bed," I said as I shut off the water, "before I do something that makes you tear the whole fucking shower down."

Neither of us bothered with a towel. We stumbled together into my room and I flung her down on the bed, chasing after her. I wanted to lick the water drops from her damp skin, but she wouldn't hold still. She pawed at me. Her fingers tangled in my hair as we kissed.

Our damp bodies should have been cold in the air conditioning, but we were a burning mess, writhing together on my bed. I didn't break the kiss as I slipped a hand under the pillow and pulled out the blindfold and rope.

"You ready?" I asked softly.

She trapped her bottom lip between her teeth, biting back a grin, and nodded quickly. God, she was sexy. I was going to miss seeing the excitement in her eyes as we both moved to get the blindfold on her, but I was looking forward to giving her this experience.

I looped the rope around her wrists and cinched them together, pulling the knot closed. "How's that?"

The word came from her breathy. "Good."

"I'm gonna tie this off on the bedframe, so I need to angle you." I tugged gently on the end of the rope, signaling how I wanted her to shift so her arms were pulled over her head.

And when it was done, I stood beside the bed and took in my work.

Nina's chest rose and fell rapidly, like she was thirsty and drinking in the air. Her gorgeous body cut a straight diagonal across the mattress, and her tanned skin stood out against the dark blue comforter. Completely bare for me except for the black blindfold. "Oh, *Nina*," I said. "You look so fucking good like that."

She shifted, subtly rubbing her legs together. It made me grin, and I fisted my cock, stroking to tease myself as I'd done to her.

Her perfect, dusty-colored nipples jutted out into points and begged for my attention. She sighed as I laid my palms on them and caressed. Her tits were amazing, and I took my time. I wasn't on anyone's schedule. No one was waiting to change setups, and I didn't have a bulleted sheet listing what acts to perform, and in which order.

She let loose a tight noise of frustration after a while. I'd been licking and pinching for a long time, roaming from one breast to the other. My lips curled into a smile. "Do you like this?"

"Yeah, I do." She shifted her hips beneath me, calling my attention to down between her legs. "But I want more."

Again she asked me for *more*, and I was thrilled. I moved along on the bed, dropping kisses over her belly, and settled between her parted thighs. Her pussy was beautiful. All pink and soft, and so wet. I traced the tip of my tongue over her clit and her whole body flinched.

"Oh!" The rope made a noise as it snapped taut, like she'd forgotten she couldn't use her hands.

I laughed darkly, and then got to work tasting her. From above, there were huge gulps of air as I licked and sucked. I teased the bud of her clit and got her bent knees to shake in response. The ache in my dick was sharp and angry, but I knew how to focus elsewhere.

Nina's back arched when I shoved my middle two fingers inside her pussy, and fluttered my tongue right above.

"Oh my God," she whined.

It just made me want to keep going. Her husky voice was loaded with sex, and to give myself some satisfaction, I rolled my hips against the bed. Yeah, dry humping the mattress wasn't something I'd do in front of cameras, or really, anyone. But Nina couldn't see under the blindfold, and I needed both hands on her. One was holding her spread open to my mouth, and the other drove deep where she was soaking wet.

"How are we doing?" I whispered. "Still all right?"

She shuddered as my lips locked onto her clit and I used suction. She gasped. "Shit, Scott. Please."

"Please, what?" Even though it was clear what

she needed.

"Fuck me," she groaned.

I crawled up her body, holding back the need to plunge deep inside as a thought popped into my head. The production companies always required a good cumshot. I wanted to go all the way and finish inside her. Fucking hell, that'd be even more intimate than kissing. I tried to keep the hopeful anticipation from changing the pitch of my voice. "No condom still okay?"

"Yeah." Her tone was clipped. "God, give it to me already."

She couldn't see the enormous grin that spread across my face. "You're demanding all of a sudden."

"Sorry." She made a face beneath the blindfold like she was embarrassed.

"What? Don't apologize." I cupped a hand to her cheek and kissed her, lowering my body over hers. Could she feel how I was throbbing as I was pressed against her?

"Not being able to see or use my hands," she whispered, "it makes me want it so bad." Her tongue darted out to swipe over her full lips, wetting them. "Scott, it makes me want *you* so bad."

And . . . I couldn't last another second. I grabbed myself by the base, steadied my dick, and sank into her. Her body was snug around me. Her mouth rounded into a silent cry of satisfaction.

Her warmth and tight fit made me hazy. I could feel every inch of her squeezing along my length, and pleasure burned up my skin. I rocked my hips into her and our moans rang out at the same time, blurring together.

I went slow.

Painstakingly slow, so we could both enjoy the feel. I'd done a lot of hard and fast, so the deliberate pace ratcheted up the intensity. Jesus, it felt good. I was so hard, and she was so wet, it was insane.

Nina's legs wrapped around my hips, wordlessly urging me to go faster, and eventually I gave into both her and my body's demands. I filled my mouth with her tits and drove into her at a blistering tempo, letting her rasping breath echo in my ear.

I fucked her . . . No, *we* fucked. Even with her hands tied down, she was right there with me, matching my desire. If anything, she seemed hungrier. More desperate.

"Oh, God," she whimpered. "Oh, oh, *oh* . . ."

Her mouth hung slack, and she arched against my chest, flattening her nipples against mine. My hands moved with a mind of their own, coursing over her naked flesh, caressing and touching. Up and down her extended arms. Over her chest, and along the length of her neck. She was so smooth and soft, and her skin was like silk.

"Yeah," Nina moaned. "*Yes*, right there."

I slammed into her, grinding against her clit, and then it happened. The rhythmic pulses of her walls clamped down, and she cried out, her hoarse voice bursting with ecstasy. Feeling her come on me was intense, and watching it was erotic. Her hands wrapped around the rope and the muscles in her upper body strained against the onslaught of pleasure.

Once again, warmth flooded through my chest. Heated satisfaction filled me as the orgasm rolled through Nina. Some actresses were great, but this orgasm, which I'd given her, was one hundred percent real. She shook beneath my body, whimpering as the sensations seemed to fade.

As she recovered, I slowed back to the slow, languid rhythm, savoring every moment of her coming. It was so fucking sexy. My lips planted kisses along her cheek, her mouth, down her neck, and along her collarbone.

Then, I began to move for me.

Deep, punishing strokes that she rose up to meet. Holy shit, was I going to be able to get her to come a second time? She squirmed around my cock like it was possible.

"I want to watch you come," she whispered abruptly.

I had to freeze. Had to hold absolutely still to avoid losing it right then, that's how hot the concept was. I tugged the blindfold off and gazed into her wide, pretty eyes as I delivered a thrust.

Then, another. And another, so deep inside her I hoped she could taste it. Heat pooled in my balls, tightening until it was unbearable. I slipped a hand under her ass and tilted her hips to meet me, and the final thrust sent me over the edge.

"Fuck, I'm coming," I said, for once not feeling pressure to stay quiet. Nina seemed to be right there with me. She latched her teeth onto her own bicep, and her eyes pinched shut for a moment as she began to come a second time. Then, her eyes blinked open and she locked her gaze onto mine.

I came harder than I ever had.

Wave after wave poured out of me, pumping into her as I exploded. It was so intense, my vision narrowed and I stopped breathing. My heart pounded as I shot into her, emptying pleasure with each surge. "Fuck, Nina. *Fuck!*"

It went on forever and shook me all the way to my core, making me collapse on top of her. My hips continued to rock as the pulsing sensations slowed and faded away. In the aftermath, I was out of breath and struggled to pull myself together.

There were strands of midnight blue in her steel-colored eyes, giving her irises depth. Goddamn, they were beautiful. My lips sealed over hers and we lay wrapped together, recovering with one passionate kiss at a time. This girl was going to do a number on me, I was certain. Now it just became a question of how I kept her coming back for *more*.

Chapter
EIGHT

I pulled open the passenger door for Nina and she got out of my truck, and then looked up at the building across the street. It was a nice night. It was warm, the sky was clear, and moonlight poured over the awning that read *Dune Nightclub*. A bouncer waited beneath, and he glanced at the IDs of the two women who strolled up to the door.

Dune wasn't the hottest club in Chicago, not by a long shot, but it did okay. There was a steady stream of customers on the weekends and the dancefloor was almost always packed. Things had perked up considerably since it came under new ownership last year.

"How often do you work here?" Nina asked.

I linked my hand with hers and pulled her toward the front door. "Usually the nights I'm not acting."

The guy at the door recognized me and waved us through. Inside, music thumped at a furious tempo and the bass pounded in my chest. The large, dark nightclub was crowded, and the bar was busier than normal, so I craned my neck to see if Joseph was back there. He sometimes had to help out us bartenders when we got slammed.

"You looking for your boss?" she yelled in my ear over the music.

I nodded.

As far as bosses went, Joseph was decent. He wasn't exactly laid back, but he was fair. He worked hard, genuinely seemed to care about his employees, and was easy to get along with. I never would have guessed what he was into, had I not let it slip once to him that I did porn.

He'd had so many questions, I wondered if he'd been trying to break into the business himself. Maybe he could have, if he was packing below the belt. He was good looking enough in his face. When he'd asked to see me alone in his office after closing time, I was concerned he was going to hit on me. No one at Dune knew if he was into chicks or dudes . . . or both.

I gently snagged the elbow of Brie, a server who had a massive hard-on for our boss. She'd know where he was, guaranteed.

"Hey, you!" Brie said, smiling. "Coming in on your night off?"

"Yeah. I'm looking for Joseph."

She glanced at Nina, down to our clasped hands, and then back to me, beaming. "Who's this?"

I'd always been an open guy, which meant Brie and I talked freely about our relationships as we cleaned tables and stocked the bar afterhours. I'd heard all about her boyfriend who seemed unable to get his shit together, and she'd listened supportively to the Kendall-Scott shitshow.

"This is Nina," I said. "My girlfriend."

After the epic sex, we'd . . . hell. We'd *cuddled* for hours talking. I'd asked her to stay in my room while I made us dinner in my messy kitchen, and then we ate frozen pizza naked in my bed. She was sexy, and smart, and funny. I didn't want the night to end.

The call came right after dinner. My friend said it was the water pump and Nina could drive the car safely to his garage, where he'd fix it in the morning.

"I like you," Nina blurted out when we got in my truck, heading for the studio.

I could have made a joke how I already knew that, given all the sex we'd had, but I heard the nervous emotion in her words, which matched what I felt.

"Can I see you again?" She seemed to swallow hard.

Seriously? "Yeah. Yes. Fuck, yes."

A huge smile broke on her face. "So, can I ask a favor?"

"Go for it."

"Don't kiss anyone else. Just me."

I was about to put the truck in gear, and paused. "You mean, when I'm acting."

"Yeah. Or, like, any other time."

My heart went all out of rhythm for a moment. God, she was almost too good to be true. I'd told her how kissing was something I didn't do unless it meant something. I'd figured after Kendall, I wouldn't be able to have a standard relationship. Eventually, I was going to meet a girl and put myself in the awkward position of choosing between her and my acting career. Was Nina telling me I could have both?

"You'd be cool with it, though?" I asked. "With me doing all the other stuff with someone else?"

She considered it. "Would you, with me?"

Pleased disbelief flooded through me, and I nodded. "As long as you don't kiss them, then yeah. I can handle it."

"Okay," she said. "Me, too."

The memory made my lips lift into a smile, but then I refocused. "Nina, this is Brie."

"Hi," Nina said.

"Joseph?" I reminded Brie.

She flashed a smile, lighting up at his name. "He went to grab another case of Bud Lite from the back."

Then, he appeared from the stockroom, a case of beer in his arms. I made my way toward him, towing Nina behind as we threaded through the crowd. Joseph set the case on the bar and one of the bartenders took it. Then, he brushed the dust off his dress shirt, turned, and peered at me. "Scott?"

"Hey, man. I know it's busy, but I wanted you to meet someone."

Joseph's gaze turned to Nina. He was older than me by at least ten years, and although he was still relatively young, he looked much more like an adult, wearing a suit without a tie. His dark hair matched his dark and curious eyes, which seemed to be evaluating Nina.

I leaned over so he could hear me. "We shot a scene together this afternoon, and Nina would like to hear more about your other club."

His surprised attention snapped to mine, and then slid back to her. I watched him drink her in. Her perfect tits, tight waist, and long legs. Even if he was gay, he could see how gorgeous she was. Joseph's expression turned warm and he looked thrilled.

"Oh, yeah?" he said. "Come on, honey, let's go upstairs

to my office and talk."

"Here's the thing, though." I shifted to stop Joseph mid-step.

"If you're looking for a finder's fee, of course I'll—"

The thought hadn't even occurred to me. I was here for her, because she wanted to know more. "No, it's just Nina and I are together now. I need to know if she works for you there, she'll be . . . safe." Safe in every sense of the word.

He almost seemed offended. "Absolutely. We have precautions in place, and excellent security." It seemed as if then he picked up on the first half of my statement. "Together how? As a couple?"

Nina nodded. He turned his skeptical expression toward me.

"We shot porn together," I reminded.

His face skewed, displeased. "That's not what this would be."

It was pretty fucking close though, he had to know that. Sex with strangers for money. "So, go upstairs and you can explain it to her. We're both okay with it."

Joseph's eyes clouded over and his jaw flexed. "You might not be working tonight, but you're still my employee, and I'd appreciate you not telling me what to do."

Whoa. I'd never seen him annoyed, but then again, I'd never flipped our boss-subordinate dynamic around, either. Was I blowing this opportunity for Nina? "Sorry, it came out wrong." I wiped my hand over my mouth, nervous. "Joseph, she's gorgeous and she fucks like a rockstar.

She'd make you both a ton of money."

His broad shoulders straightened as if letting the tension roll out of his body. "I can tell you're at least right about the first part." He focused on her, and his tone softened. "You're a very beautiful woman."

The club was dimly lit, but the blush that spread across her face was plain to see. "Thank you," she said.

Joseph blinked at her surprisingly deep voice, and then his lips peeled back into a smile. "You're welcome. How about we all go upstairs and talk?" He gestured toward the doorway that led to the stairs, then his exacting gaze settled back on me. "You can watch her audition, and then we'll see how *okay* everyone is feeling."

Joseph led the way, so he didn't see her reach for my hand as we walked across the dancefloor. That tiny gesture reaffirmed she was okay, and when she smiled at me, I saw her eyes brimming with excitement.

Oh, yeah. We were going to be a helluva lot better than just okay.

We were going to have so much fun together.

CONTINUE READING WITH

THREE SIMPLE RULES

&

THREE HARD LESSONS

ONE *more* RULE

THE BLINDFOLD CLUB
NOVELLA 2.5

Chapter ONE

PAYTON

Dominic's arm wrapped around my waist, steadying me as the train rocketed around a corner. He clung with one hand to the gray strap overhead, while I used my knees to keep our bags from tumbling over. His luggage slammed painfully into my thigh. The anxiety-inducing thirteen-hour flight from Tokyo had gotten to me.

"I hate riding the El," I said, "when I own an expensive and fucking beautiful car."

Dominic gave a tight smile. "Which is downtown and doesn't have room for your luggage."

"Sure it does. There just wouldn't be room for you."

His fingers flicked me playfully just inside of my hipbone, where the tattoo rested beneath my jeans. He did it whenever I made a joke about our relationship, his wordless reminder of how much I really loved him.

"You better watch it."

"Or what?" I had my hand on his chest and drummed my fingers, challenging his seduction right back.

His embrace tightened further, and his mouth was right by my ear. "Didn't you tell me once you wanted to reenact the scene from *Risky Business*?"

My face warmed with a smile. I'd suggested that almost a year ago on a Japanese train, but it felt like a lifetime now. Dominic had turned down my offer, worried he'd lose his riding privileges, and I'd learned during my year in Tokyo just how important those were.

Now we were on an elevated train barreling for downtown Chicago, just like the movie.

Well, not exactly. It was midafternoon, and the car was packed, standing room only. I glanced at the bored faces of the travelers around us and shrugged. "I'm game if you are."

"Fuck, Payton, you'd love that, wouldn't you?" His infectious laugh sounded so good, I'd never grow tired of listening to it.

The city we would call home again in three months loomed in the distance. Chicago. Dark, dirty, loud, and everything I wanted. I'd missed the gorgeous skyline, and from Dominic's expression, I could tell he had too.

Once we hit the loop, we got off, lugged our bags down the steps, and headed out onto the sidewalk.

"It feels like we've been gone for years," I said, glancing down the street.

It had been February when Dominic had flown across the world, determined for us to be together, no matter what. Going back to Japan with him was a choice I'd made even before he proposed. Now it was September, and our best friends were getting married.

"Which way is the lake?" I said, exhausted and disoriented. "Did they move it while we were gone?"

"I don't think so." Dominic motioned toward the left.

"Are you guessing, or do you know?" I was giving him

attitude when I didn't mean to be. "Fuck, I'm tired."

His expression was amused. "It's four blocks this way, devil woman. I looked it up while we were at baggage claim waiting for the suitcases."

All of our time together, and I still wasn't accustomed to his planning. I liked flying by the seat of my pants, making split decisions. Dominic enjoyed thinking ahead.

My suitcase wheels rattled over a grate as I followed beside him. "You love this."

"Having a clue? Yeah."

We hit the lobby of the Opulent Hotel right at three, so we could check in, and I sighed against him during the elevator ride up to our room. "What's the plan again?"

"We'll take a nap to get over some of the jet lag, then meet Evie and Logan for dinner."

"Evelyn," I corrected. It was an inside joke now. He had every right to call her by the nickname, but I loved to tease. The lit floor numbers ticked by as we climbed, bringing us closer and closer to sleep. I could hardly keep my eyes open. "Where are we meeting them?"

"Benihana."

The Japanese restaurant? I'd sell my Jaguar F-Type just for some American food. "Fuck off, we are not."

Dominic's smirk at his joke almost melted my panties. "You're so sexy when you're pissed."

The elevator doors peeled open, and we trekked along the carpet until he had the room door open for me. No need to bother with the lights. Luggage was left by the closet as I went to the curtains and dragged them closed. I tugged off my shirt and tossed it on the chair in the corner, then stripped out of my jeans.

I locked eyes with my fiancé across the room as he began to shed his clothes. A triumphant smile quirked on his lips.

"What?" Was I acting strange? He was looking at me like I was hilarious, when all I was doing was getting ready for was a coma.

"Nothing." His rough voice cut through the darkened room. "Just thinking about the last time we were in a hotel, trying to get some sleep during the day."

I was pulling the cover off and froze mid-action.

"You fought me about getting into bed together," he added. His pants fell off his hips, leaving him in only his boxers, and he came to me, brushing my hair off my shoulder.

"Yeah," I said in a hushed voice. "Last time, I wanted to fuck you, not sleep with you."

His lips skimmed over the curve of my neck, drawing a shudder from my body. "Not true now?"

He loved holding that over me, just one of the many battles he'd won. I couldn't sleep *without* him now. And yes, I was tired. Two seconds ago my answer would have been I'd rather sleep than screw. But Dominic's touch lit me up and made me burn. "I always want you, Dominic, even after we've been up for nineteen hours."

His lips sealed over mine, and hands tangled in the straps of my bra, tugging them down. The smooth skin of his chest pressed against mine as his arms encased me.

Kissing him was insane. When his tongue filled my mouth, I moved mine against it, moaning into the kiss.

"Well," he said, ending it abruptly, "calm down. I need to sleep."

A fucking bluff. My gaze dropped to his boxers, which were tented. I shrugged and faked indifference. "You don't need to be awake for this. I can get what I need."

A startled cry tore from my throat as he tossed me sideways onto the bed, bent over me, and pressed the length of his cock against my center. Only our underwear held us back.

"Is this what you need?" The gravel of his voice was more pronounced when he whispered.

I clawed at him, my nails digging in. "*Yes.*"

Dominic slid down my body, his hot mouth coursing a line over my belly. "So, my tongue couldn't get the job done?" He worked lower and lower, tugging the crotch of my panties to the side.

"It can get the job started," I whispered. Cool air wafted over my exposed flesh, but only intensified the ache for him.

He hovered, teasing kisses and touches on the inside of my thighs. *Fuck*, I needed his mouth on me. This last week, he'd had to work late every night. A drawer full of vibrators didn't compare to my man. I pushed a hand into his soft, fawn-colored hair, urging him to taste me with his wicked tongue.

"What do you want?" he whispered against my skin.

"Fuck me with your mouth."

Bliss rolled up my legs as Dominic's tongue licked over my clit. I had one hand in his hair and the other on the sheet beneath me, and both clenched into fists. My lungs squeezed as a finger plunged inside, taking my pleasure up another level.

He knew exactly how I liked it, but didn't give it to me. His slowly thrusting finger was just a little too gentle, his tongue too hesitant. Teasing. Holding me exactly where he wanted me, right at the edge.

I grew lightheaded and scored my nails over his scalp, desperate for more. He could hear my whimper, begging him without words, but he ignored it. He wanted me to come at his pace, and Dominic was used to getting his way.

I endured his deliberate mouth for a lifetime.

Once my legs began to shake, he kicked into a new gear, flooring my accelerator. His urgent sucking, licking, biting . . . Two fingers speared into me, filling and stretching in an ache that burned so good. I was about to come, just as he wanted.

"God, please," I moaned, shivering as the waves of the orgasm built.

"*Zutto issho ni itai*," he said in Japanese. "*I want to be with you forever.*"

I cried out, a strangled sound that died as I burst open. My quivering thighs locked around his head. Oh God, it was good. He was so perfect, from his stunning blue eyes to his desire to give me exactly what I needed. Liquid heat flamed through me, leaving warmth behind.

My legs went boneless as panties were yanked down.

Dominic stood, and before I could catch my breath, his hands scooped beneath my knees and pulled me to the edge of the bed, sliding me across the sheets. I clutched at his hips when his thick cock sank into me.

"Yes," I breathed. "I love you."

My left hand walked up his chest, and my engagement ring glinted in the sunlight the hotel curtains couldn't block. I rose up on an elbow, and my grip curled around the back of his neck. I needed him closer, his lips on mine.

His first slow thrust was deep and my toes tensed into points. I arched my back as I pulled his face down, slamming our lips together. Connecting with the love of my life on all levels. His hardened chest flattened against mine, pushing my breasts into him as his thrusts increased in intensity.

"I love you," he whispered, raining kisses along my jawline. "Real."

It didn't take long for his tempo to erase my mind and burn away all my exhaustion. My only desire was for him to reach the same climax he'd already given me. Not like it mattered. He wouldn't settle for just one orgasm from my body. He'd go until he had me screaming, and only then would he worry about himself.

"Goddamnit," he groaned, watching me writhe beneath him. I palmed my breast with my right hand, rolling and pinching the nipple between my fingers, and Dominic's pupils dilated with lust. "So fucking hot."

"You're gonna make me come again."

"Good." Hips beat into mine, his cock growing harder

as the volume of my moans increased.

"But, shit, you make it impossible to be quiet."

The sapphire eyes gleamed. "Who said you had to be quiet? I know I sure as hell didn't."

"We're . . . in a hotel." It was a challenge not to pant it out.

"And?" He ground his pelvis against my clit, and flashes of electricity danced up my spine.

"People will think you're murdering me again."

His perfect smile spread across his face. "I'm still hazy about that. Did they think I was killing you with my cock? Yeah, you were screaming about it, but how—"

I lifted up on my elbows again and latched my teeth on the side of his neck, drawing a sharp noise of surprise, laced with an edge of pain. It flipped a switch in him. Sweet, playful Dominic went away, replaced by the darker, aggressive version.

"That's how it's going to be?" he asked in his rough voice. "All right, let me help you be quiet, slut."

He bolted upright, drawing out of me, and the sudden emptiness was shocking. I blinked up at him. Was he really going to stop just because I'd nipped at his neck? I hadn't even left a mark. In fact, I'd never left a mark on him, other than the tattoo on his hip, which had been his idea. He'd marked me plenty of times, not that I was complaining. We both knew how much that turned me on.

When I sat up, chasing after him, a hand gripped my shoulder and pushed me to turn around.

"On your back," he ordered. "Head hanging off the

edge of the bed."

I shivered with excitement. I loved his dominant side, which had expanded under Akira's masterful teaching. I scrambled in my eagerness to follow his command, pivoting on my ass and scooting down to lie flat on the mattress.

"Open your mouth so I can fuck it."

My pussy clenched at his dirty words. I barely got my lips open and he was there, sliding his dick inside, wet with my own taste. At this angle, he could drive deep into my throat. I swirled my tongue over him, getting him to pulse, and there wasn't anything else like that sensation. Knowing how much he enjoyed what I was doing to him. I wrapped one hand around his cock, twisting my fist around him as he thrust in and out.

My other hand trailed down between my legs where I was needy and unsatisfied. And no sooner had I started playing with myself than he leaned over me, seized my wrist, and pushed it away.

"No, no, no," he teased. "We don't want you getting too loud."

I wanted to remind him that he had my mouth occupied, but he dropped my hand at my breast, squeezing down on it.

"You can play with these," Dominic said, dragging our hands over my tits. "But this," his fingers glided down through my wet pussy and slapped my sensitive flesh, "this is fucking *mine*."

His other hand was a fist, and he set it beside my hip, so he had leverage as he leaned over and sawed his cock in my greedy mouth, slow enough to not gag me. When I tightened my grip, he groaned in approval, and the fingers on my clit rubbed faster. I bucked under his skilled touch.

Compatible wasn't a strong enough word for us. It wasn't like every time we had sex it was the most amazing rapture ever. But we always clicked. Always worked together. Even our mediocre sex was fun and enjoyable. I hoped I'd never take a minute of him for granted.

A rough finger shoved inside me, and I moaned while he was lodged in my throat. "Mmm..."

"*Fuck.*" It came out strained. The vibration of my moan must have felt pretty damn good, judging by his reaction. The heel of his palm pressed against my clit while the finger fucked me in time with his hips. Pleasure built at the base of my spine, teasing the orgasm again.

I pumped my fist on him. Used suction. Spun the edge of my tongue on the head of his dick. Everything in my arsenal to bring him to the brink, as he was about to tip me over into ecstasy.

"Shit. Oh, fuck, yes," Dominic said between deep breaths. "Take it."

It was the last push I needed to release, and I exploded. My cries were muffled by his enormous, throbbing cock, and as I came, my legs trembling, it was the wordless permission he needed.

Breath left him in a loud burst, and his movements became jerky and erratic, followed by a long noise of satisfaction, which rumbled up from deep in his chest. He came in spurts, wave after wave, filling my mouth, and when he ceased, I swallowed. It drew another low moan from him.

"Payton," he whispered, his knuckles brushing over my cheekbone. He stepped back and helped me sit up. In a heartbeat, he was seated beside me on the bed, his arms trapping me. I tilted my head so he could trace kisses along my neck, my eyes falling shut and my fingertips gritting over his unshaven face.

His kisses slowed, and reality returned, one layer after another. I blinked sluggishly. We collapsed on the bed and Dominic tugged the sheet up over our sweat-dampened bodies.

A chuckle rang out when I curled up beside him, needing the contact against his warm body. I sighed dramatically, but since he couldn't see my face, I grinned. We'd pushed each other into new territory. Talking. Sleeping in the same bed. Love.

Soon, marriage.

"Hey." I rolled over onto my other hip, turning to face him. "Let's get married."

His eyes were already closed, one hand tucked under his pillow. "Thought we already agreed on that."

"No," I said. "Let's get married while we're home. Tomorrow."

Chapter TWO

Dominic's eyes flew open and a scowl darkened his face. "What?"

As the idea began to take shape, I grew more excited. "We've been living together for a year. The paperwork with our work visas is a pain in the ass. We could go to the courthouse and do one of those quickie Justice of the Peace things."

His face was stoic, but the muscles beneath his jaw tensed, as if clenching his teeth. He wasn't a fan of this idea?

"Have you ever been to any of the Cook County courthouses?" He asked it in a lazy voice, but there was tension beneath. "Because if you had, I don't think you'd be chomping at the bit to go back."

"Okay, the courthouse isn't great, but it's not *that* bad. Think about it—"

His expression turned serious. "I already have."

I hesitated as the words sank in. He'd considered getting married while we were home, but decided against it. "And . . .?"

"This is Evie and Logan's wedding, not ours."

"Seriously? We don't even have to tell anyone. Just you and me." My fingers brushed over his jaw, cupping his face. "I'm tired of waiting, and I don't need the big party or the dress. I want to be your wife."

He blinked slowly, and I saw the thought run through his gorgeous eyes. He wanted this too, and badly, but he shook his head. "I really fucking want that, but there are a bunch of reasons why we should wait."

"Yeah?" I deflated somewhat. "Convince me this isn't the best idea ever."

"Our families won't like it."

I raised an eyebrow. Of course it mattered what Dominic's family thought, because they were warm and fuzzy, and the way a family was supposed to be. Besides his sweet parents, I was getting two hilarious sisters-in-law in the deal. I was less interested in what my family had to say about any decision I made in my life.

"I know your family might not like it," I said, "but they'll get over it. I have zero fucks to give about my family."

They'd met Dominic only once, via Skype, in a super awkward ten-minute conversation. That was all the time my selfish parents could spare for the man who wanted to marry their only daughter. Dominic and I had booked our plane tickets months ago for Evie's wedding, in the same fucking city where my parents lived, and still, plans to meet face-to-face were up in the air. I'd sort of stopped trying to make it happen, and I'd bet on my life that we'd fly back to Tokyo without seeing them. *"Sorry, Payton, I wish we could, but it's been such a hectic week,"* I could already hear my mother saying.

"Next," I demanded.

"Your parents said they'd pay for the wedding."

I practically snorted. "See, we'd be saving them money."

He ran a hand over my hip, then fingertips traced in the hollow of my back. "You could invite everyone from the club." The way he delivered the statement was odd. There was some sort of meaning I wasn't picking up on, and his expression turned devious. "I thought you'd love that, your ultra conservative parents footing the bill for dinner and an open bar for a bunch of high-class escorts."

"Oh my God." I couldn't stop the grin. "You're right, I do love that. Fuck, I'm such a bitch." And I wasn't even sorry about it.

"Don't get me wrong, devil woman." The fingertips skimmed up over my shoulder blades, all the way until he tucked a lock of hair behind my ear and cupped my face. "You know I want to give you whatever you want, and I'm so fucking glad that happens to include my last name. But I think *I* want the party, and the dress, and all that shit. I want everyone there to celebrate with us, and see how incredibly lucky I am."

I felt warm and giddy inside, but I couldn't let on how much his words affected me. Whenever things grew serious, my immediate response was sarcasm to cover my vulnerability. So I faked disdain. "You're *such* a romantic."

"And maybe I just want a wedding so afterward I can tear the dress off of my wife on our wedding night and fuck her like the dirty girl she is."

I closed the space between us, kissing him sweetly. "Shit, Dominic, you should have led with that. If that's what you want, that's what I want, too."

※

The alarm on Dominic's phone began chiming at seven, and we stumbled to the shower together, bleary-eyed. Even though it was nine in the morning tomorrow in Japan, the three-hour nap hadn't done much to recharge.

"I saw a Walgreens a block away," Dominic said as he scrubbed shampoo into his hair. "We can grab some Red Bull and slam it in the cab on our way to the restaurant."

"Can I mainline it?"

We hurried to get dressed. Dominic pulled on a French blue button-down shirt with the sleeves rolled back and black pants. The shirt matched the color of his eyes and showed off the watch I'd bought him.

I tugged the hem down of my seafoam green dress and slipped my feet into a sexy pair of nude heels. Then I donned my chandelier earrings and tousled my hair once more. "You ready?"

"I'm waiting for you to ask me something."

What . . . ? *Oh.* I loved this game. How the fuck had I forgotten? I strolled over to him, hooking my fingers through his belt loops and pulling his lower body tight against mine. "Do I have your permission to wear panties tonight . . . Sir?"

His expression was victory mixed with desire. "I'll allow it for now." His kiss was hungry and over too soon. "You look beautiful tonight," he whispered.

His compliment threw me off balance, but in a great way. I struggled to recover and cracked the joke, "I always look beautiful."

"That's what I love most about you."

"How humble I am?"

It came out serious. "No, that you look almost as good as I do. Your personality's not important."

I flicked him on his hip, hitting his tattoo that matched mine.

We did exactly as Dominic had suggested and drank Red Bull on our way to the Italian restaurant, which was packed with people. I clung to his thick arm as we wove through the crowd and headed up the stairs to where Logan had texted us the table was located.

Evie looked flat out gorgeous. A pre-wedding glow, perhaps. Her excitement at marrying Logan was like a filter, making everything seem brighter and better. Would I be like this the final days before marrying Dominic? I already felt that way.

I hugged her fiercely. "Fuck, I missed you."

She smiled as she pulled back. "Right back at you."

We turned to watch our fiancés shake hands, which seemed too formal, but I had the feeling Logan wasn't the hugging type. Which was exactly why I stepped up and wrapped my arms around him. He went rigid in my embrace and his gaze shifted to Dominic, worried. It made me choke back a laugh. Yeah, I'd had sex with Logan, but I knew Dominic was comfortable with this. I'd made it crystal clear to my future husband that he was all I ever wanted. And it was so much fun to see typically composed Logan uncomfortable.

I squeezed a hand on Logan's shoulder. "You remember what I said?"

"That if I'm late to the wedding, you'll rip off my dick and shove it up my ass?" Logan's intense eyes blinked, unfazed. "No, I'd forgotten. Please tell me again."

"If anyone's going to be late," Evie said, "I think we know who that'll be." She gestured to herself.

Logan gave me a serious look. "I'm counting on you to get her there on time. She has this way of making you think she's on schedule, and then drops the bomb ten minutes before departure that she wants to take a quick shower."

Evie snorted. "One time, Logan. And why, exactly, did I need the shower?"

Logan's gaze drifted up to the left as he recalled the memory, and a half-smile bowed on his lips. He tugged her close to him and whispered something. It was hard to hear in the noisy restaurant, but sounded like, "Because you were dirty."

We sat, ordered drinks, and chitchatted about random things. Our flight, their jobs, the wedding. Dominic's arm rested comfortably on the back of my chair, his thumb brushing patterns on my shoulder.

Evie wore a sleeveless black dress that draped in the front and hung low to give a peek at her cleavage. She was a beautiful woman, and although Logan was attractive, he was lucky to have her. Evie fucking rocked. When I'd quit my job at Rosso Media Group and began working at the club, she hadn't judged me. Nor did she abandoned me, or try to talk me out of it as some of my other friends had. Evie *got* me.

And that was probably what I liked most about Logan. He treated her as if she were everything, even with the way he looked at her. She was the center of his goddamn universe. My final night as a working girl at the club, I'd been on the table wishing I could find a connection to someone just a fraction as strong as what they had.

In walked Dominic, and boom. Done.

The conversation floated from topic to topic easily, like no time had passed with us being apart. There was a pang in my stomach. I already knew I'd spend my first week back in Tokyo being fucking homesick. *Just three more months.*

"What are the plans tonight?" Evie asked, her attention focused on me. "Or do we not get to know them?"

An evil grin warmed my face, and beneath the table, I squeezed Dominic's knee. We spoke at the same time. "It's a surprise."

I dug into my purse, pulled out the tiara I'd bought, and set it on the table. It was decorated with plastic penises, and everyone stared at it, the peach colored cocks on springs waving comically.

"Don't worry, Logan," Dominic deadpanned. "That's for Evie."

"Evelyn," I corrected, but Dominic just smirked.

Logan raised an eyebrow and his attention swung to his fiancé, his voice teasing. "Still remember what they look like?"

Evie's face flushed as she clenched the tiara in her hand and set it in her lap, hiding it from view. "Ha, ha, boss."

Well, that was weird. "What do you mean?"

"Nothing, don't worry about it." My friend's voice was high and rushed. Apparently she hadn't gotten any better at lying since I'd left Chicago.

"Oh, no. Tell me, or you put the Princess Penis crown on right now."

The men chuckled, but I was entirely serious, and it was obvious from Evie's nervous look she knew. A deep breath was sucked in. She tucked a lock of hair behind an ear, straightened her shoulders, and gave me a plain look.

"I told Logan no more sex before the wedding."

Chapter
THREE

For a moment, sound fell from the room. I couldn't focus my thoughts. "What the fuck? Why?"

"Because," she snapped, "I want our wedding night to be special, okay? I liked the idea of building the anticipation, and I thought no sex or nudity would do that."

"Shit, no nudity either?" Dominic's voice was thinly veiled horror. Was he worried I'd like this concept and want to do something similar? It sounded like fucking torture.

Logan had a pained smile, as if it were humorous and awful at the same time. "Yeah. She changes in our bathroom or the closet with the door shut."

"When did the rule go into effect?" I asked Evie, who stared at her shrimp appetizer.

There was no hesitation from Logan. "Thirty seven days ago."

Oh. My. God. Dominic and I exchanged glances. How was this going to affect our plans?

Her voice was soft. "I didn't make the rule to punish us."

Logan shifted in his seat, leaning into her as he radiated concern. "Hey, I know that. I don't know if *like* is the right word, but I understand the rule. You know I won't break it." His fingers curled under her chin and tilted her up into a soft kiss. "I did think you'd cave by now, though, naughty girl. You hardly ever follow the rules."

Their intimate moment forced me to turn to Dominic. "No sex for thirty-seven days. I might die."

He scowled. "That's nothing. Try going a fucking *year*."

I pressed my lips together to hold back the giggle. He'd gone that long without sex when he'd first moved to Japan, before we met. "Oh, yeah. Poor Dominic. We made up for lost time, though."

"We're still making up for it. There are at least a dozen inches in our apartment where I haven't fucked you yet."

"It's so spacious," I said of our microscopic place. "I don't know how we'll get it done in the next three months."

Our server delivered our dinners, and once she was gone, I went needling for clarification. "The no nudity rule only applies to you two, right?"

Logan glanced to Evie, probably trying to conceal his hopefulness.

"Yeah," she said. "If Dominic wants to take Logan to a strip club, that's—"

I giggled. "Slut, I wasn't asking for him."

We finished dinner, and although Evie pried for more information, Dominic and I stayed tight-lipped. He received the text message we were waiting for just a few minutes after he'd paid the bill, and we escorted the bride and groom toward the lobby.

"You drive?" Dominic's question was directed to Logan.

"No, is that a problem?"

I shook my head as I pushed through the front door.

"Nope, it's perfect." I strolled toward the black stretch limo that was pulled up out front, and enjoyed the curious looks of the people on the sidewalk.

The stout driver wore a black suit and a friendly smile. "Mrs. Ward?"

I grinned. "Yeah, someday. Are you Saul?" When he nodded, I added, "Awesome. Hope you're ready for a wild night."

Saul smoothed a hand over his dark hair and flashed an easy smile. "Whatever you say, ma'am."

"You got a limo?" Evie's eyes were wide, scanning the length of black tinted windows.

"Fuck yeah, we did," I said. Saul hurried to open the back door, and I gestured to my best friend. "In you go." She ducked inside, and I glanced at Logan. "Now you, Stone."

Logan's dark eyes narrowed the slightest bit before he followed her. Yeah, he didn't like being bossed around, and he probably didn't like being in the dark about the plans. I stifled my chuckle. He was about to be a whole lot more in the dark.

I climbed in, sliding across the back bench and Dominic's impressive form was beside me a moment later, seated on the black leather. The ceiling was lit with silver LED lights, which sparkled and winked like stars. Logan and Evie were perched on the side bench, facing the bar where a bottle of champagne was holstered in the ice bucket.

"You guys didn't have to do this," she said, playing it cool, but I could tell how much this meant to her, and I was thrilled. She deserved it.

And even though it was Dominic's money that was paying for the night, I'd helped him plan. This limo had been my suggestion, as had been our first stop, so I dug into my purse and found what I was looking for.

Dominic reached for the champagne when the limo eased its way into traffic. "Of course we did," he said. "It's not every day Logan decides to get married." His gravel voice had an upswing of teasing to it, then dipped back into serious territory. "I didn't think he'd ever get hitched, but obviously he was waiting for you."

A warm expression flitted through Evie's eyes as my fiancé popped the cork on the bottle with a dull thump. Logan looked pleased, grabbed a crystal tumbler off the bar, and held it ready. Golden champagne was poured. The glass was passed to Evie, and as soon as it was done, I tore open the plastic wrap in my hands and handed her something else.

Her blue eyes scanned the black blindfold and she licked her lips. Was it in anxiety or excitement? Or was she thinking about the last time I'd handed her a blindfold, and the scorching hot threesome that had ensued? Her fingers brushed mine as she took it. It was impossible not to think about, but it had to be worse for her. She was the one who'd gone more than a month without sex.

"And for you, Logan." I tugged open the second wrapper and held it out for him.

He stared at the blindfold as if wary, and his gaze flicked to Dominic, who shrugged like he had no idea what was going to happen, even though he did.

The soon-to-be newlyweds locked gazes, communicating through a wordless conversation. Evie let out a breath, then slipped the blindfold on, tugging it over her closed eyes. Logan hesitated, but Dominic's indifferent attitude while he continued to pour drinks seemed to do the trick.

"I feel like a fucking idiot," Logan said when he had it over his eyes.

"Well, you look great," Dominic joked. "And don't worry, Payton and I aren't going to get naked and fuck or anything now." Even under the blindfold, Logan didn't seem thrilled. "I'm handing you your champagne—"

A hand reached for it at the exact moment Dominic moved, knocking the glass and champagne sloshed over the side, splashing Logan.

"Fuck, watch it." Dominic's voice was amused. He used his other hand to guide Logan's to the glass.

"It would be easier if I could see."

"Where's the fun in that?" I said.

It was a short ride to the Baton Lounge, but probably felt longer to Evie and Logan. After the initial uncomfortable moments wore off, it seemed to relax both of them. Like it did to me, putting a restriction on them made them feel more open. No pressure to do anything. *Just sit back,* I thought, *and let me and Dominic take charge.*

Maneuvering them out of the limo while they were still wearing the blindfolds was fun. As Evie stood on the sidewalk, I set the crown of cocks on her head, working to get it to sit right.

"Yeah," she said. "Make sure it's on straight, because it would be so embarrassing if it was crooked."

I looped my arm through hers and urged her forward, keeping her from stumbling as we went in through the open door. There was a loud bang, a noise of pain, and I turned to see Logan backing away, as if he'd run into the pane of glass beside the entrance.

"Oh," Dominic said. "Watch out, there's a door ahead." He grinned, clearly enjoying busting Logan's balls.

"What the hell, Dominic?" Logan demanded.

Evie's face contorted with worry. "Are you okay?"

"He's fine," I said.

It was muttered by Logan, but still loud enough for me to hear. "Asshole." His hands searched, then grasped a shoulder, letting Dominic guide him.

The large room had tiered seating with tables, and a stage along the back wall. The woman just inside the door scanned the tickets on my phone, and didn't seem to care about Evie's tiara or blindfold. She did, however, stare at Dominic like he was naked. It was both annoying and kind of an ego boost. This stranger lusted after him, and could I really fault her for that? That night I'd met Dominic, I'd thought he was crazy good-looking, and time only made him hotter.

"You're in the front row," she said, her glittering eyes never leaving him. "Your server can help you find the table."

Like it was really that hard.

We had our friends seated at the table and ordered

drinks before we let them take off their blindfolds. "Give them back to me," I said over the din of the crowd. "This is just our first stop."

"Where are we?" Logan glanced around, evaluating his surroundings. "And why are Dominic and I the only guys here?"

He was right, the audience was ninety-nine percent female. I laughed. "Trust me, you're not the only guys here."

It was at that precise moment the plus-sized host took the stage, wearing a sparkling blue dress and a heavy coat of makeup. She strolled up to the microphone, brushed her long dark red hair over her shoulder, and gave us a sexy look.

"Good evening, ladies. I'm your host, Ginger."

If the glitzy dress and overdone makeup hadn't already done it, the deep voice was what clued Logan in.

"Is that a—"

"Drag queen?" Dominic answered. "Oh, yeah."

Logan's gaze bounced between the performer on stage, to Dominic, and back again. He had to be wondering what the hell they were doing here.

"I made a deal with Dominic," I said. "We stick together tonight. This is what I wanted for Evie, and we'll get to yours later. Sorry."

The truth was I trusted Dominic, and hell, I trusted Logan too, to keep their dicks in their pants during their bachelor party. But who I didn't trust, was other people. I'd had bachelor parties come through the blindfold club, and I'd seen things escalate beyond what anyone intended.

Plus, the girl drooling over Dominic when we first walked in only affirmed my decision. It would be easier for him to brush off any unwanted attention if I was right beside him.

The show began. It was one female impersonator's set right after another. Gorgeous dresses, fake tits, and tuck jobs that were fucking magic. They danced, lip-synced to Lady Gaga and Whitney Houston, and took tips from the female audience, who treated them to catcalls and cheers. The show was a riot.

Our men sat, transfixed. Curious, but trying not to display it.

"Holy shit." It came from Evie when a blonde stepped on stage in five-inch heels and a mini-skirt. "He has nicer legs than I do."

By the time the final number was over, we were all buzzing from our drinks, and uptight, control freak Logan sort of looked relaxed. Perhaps it was Evie's hand resting high on his thigh, lingering close to the danger zone.

After we filed out of the Baton Lounge, we mobbed with the rest of the crowd in the warm September night, and strolled slowly down the block to where our limo waited. We ducked inside one by one.

"That was awful," Dominic said, a smile twisting on his sexy lips. "The ones that were obviously dudes were fine, but the other ones . . ."

I giggled. "Your dick get confused?"

His arm hooked around my shoulders and pulled me close. "Be quiet, devil woman."

"Or?"

"Spankings." His lip curled in a half-smile.

I played up my eagerness by batted my eyelashes. "Now?"

"Well, we'll get their blindfolds back on first."

"Oh, of course."

Our friends stared at us like they were unsure if we were serious. I knew Dominic wasn't, but if he wanted to . . . he certainly knew I was game. Instead, I retrieved the blindfolds and passed them out.

Logan looked even less excited about it this time around. "Calm down." I motioned for him to put it on. "The only queen for the rest of the night is the one wearing the cock crown."

His head swung toward Evie. "It does look great on you."

"Thanks, boss. Should I wear it to work on Monday?"

"Sure. That wouldn't be an HR nightmare."

They put their masks on at the same time, and like me, Evie curled up under her fiancé's arm, snuggling close, one hand on Logan's chest. His fingers stroked up and down her bare arm. She tucked in further, putting her lips against his neck.

The gentle, sweet kiss she'd started grew when he turned his head into hers, bringing their mouths together. It was like she'd struck a match and set Logan on fire, and although it was probably weird as hell for me to watch our friends making out, I did it anyway. I'd spent more than a year at the club and had seen every sexual act done in a wide range of ways. But the way Evie's needy hands clutched at his shirt while he devoured her kiss was so fucking sexy.

His hands reached out, finding her hips, and then he pulled her into his lap so she was straddling him. The skirt of her dress rode up on her thighs, and Dominic's gaze automatically turned out the window.

"Such a gentleman," I whispered to him, knowing he was probably blushing. Just another thing I loved about him.

A soft sigh came from Evie, drawing my attention back to the couple. She was rocking in his lap, her hands cupping the sides of his jaw. His arms were tight around her back, holding her as their kiss grew more intense.

"This is dangerous, naughty girl."

"Why?" Her voice was low and sultry. "We've still got our clothes on and you can't see anything."

"I'm not worried about me."

Her grip fell away from his face and her back straightened. "You think I can't resist you after just some kissing?"

Below Logan's black blindfold, his lips peeled back in a smile. "You did mention it was your gateway drug."

"Give me some credit. I bet I can handle it better than you can."

His laugh said exactly how foolish he thought she was being. "Doubtful."

Oh, this was about to get interesting. Evie was focused and driven. She hated to lose, and she'd told me Logan was the same. I could sense the challenge coming.

She sat perfectly still as his lips skimmed over her

neck, trailing kisses. "You seem awfully sure of yourself, Logan."

"If I wanted you to break your rule, we know I could get you to do it."

She pulled even further back from him. "Oh, do we? By all means, boss, go ahead and try."

Logan took a deep breath. "You sure?"

"I'm sure you're overly confident, yeah."

"All right, Evie." Logan smiled. "Challenge accepted."

Chapter FOUR

Saul parked the limo in front of a liquor store, and we left our blindfolded friends in the back while Dominic and I hurried in to pick up drinks.

"Champagne, whiskey, and rum," Dominic said to the clerk when we entered the tiny shop. He whipped out his wallet a second later and retrieved his credit card.

"What's the rush?" I asked.

"Gotta hurry before Evie caves and they're fucking in the back of the limo."

I latched a hand on Dominic's forearm, stilling him. "Evelyn. And what the hell makes you think that'll happen?"

The card was swiped, a receipt signed, and he hauled the paper bag of bottles into his arms. "Because I know Logan. He plays to win."

"Yeah, well, so does Evie."

The sapphire eyes sharpened on me. "Sorry, she doesn't stand a chance, but you want to make it interesting?"

My gaze narrowed to match his. "I'm listening."

"If Evie reverses her rule before, I dunno, say sunrise tomorrow . . ." Dominic's jaw ticked as he seemed to assemble the thought in his head. "You call your parents and try again to get a dinner or something between us worked out."

I groaned. *Of course.* "I don't know why you're making a big deal out of that. Seriously, you're not missing much with my folks. I have to force them to make time, you really want to spend two hours with people who don't want to be there?"

His expression was fixed. "Do I want to meet my in-laws before the wedding? Yeah, Payton, I do."

"Fine. And if Logan breaks the rule and asks to have sex?"

He yanked open the shop door and held it for me. "Name your terms, devil woman."

What did I want that Dominic wouldn't give me freely? There was nothing. Sure, I'd like to skip the whole big wedding, but no way in hell was I going to deny him that. Then the thought formed in my mind. He'd been resistant to one request I'd made . . . "You and I have lunch with Joseph this week."

We strode toward the limo, and tension tightened Dominic's broad shoulders. Normally, I liked his possessiveness over me, but not where Joseph was concerned, because Joseph was my friend. A good friend. Yes, we'd fucked a bunch of times, but it had been empty sex for both of us, and stopped the moment Dominic walked into my life.

"Okay, you got it." Dominic tugged open the limo door. "But just know, you're gonna lose."

Really? I glared at him, but didn't bother to respond, and slid into the backseat. "What the fuck are you doing? Hands to yourselves!"

Evie and Logan scattered like teenagers caught in the act by parents, and Evie let out a nervous laugh. She probably thought I was kidding and giving her a hard time, but I was serious. The way Evie talked about kissing Logan made it sound like he could get her to do almost anything. Pre-Dominic, I thought she was crazy. Now I sort of understood.

Fuck, I did not want have to call my mom again.

Bass thumped repeatedly from beyond the black door that led into the club. We stood in the anteroom while Dominic paid our group's cover charge, and I pretended not to notice the bouncer's lewd stare.

Dominic's hand was abruptly on my ass, sliding over to rest on my opposite hip, and his scowl was directed at the bouncer. His possessiveness was showing in all its brilliant colors. I adjusted the paper bag in my arms, and the bottles clinked. "I can fuck you right here, if that will help."

Evie's mouth fell open. "Are you talking to me?" With the blindfold still on, she couldn't tell it was meant for Dominic.

"No, sorry." I laughed and helped her toward the entrance. She had one hand on my shoulder and the other laced with Logan's, but he was surprisingly quiet. *Shit.* "You know where we are, Logan?"

"The bottles gave it away."

Chicago had an ordinance banning alcohol from being

served at the same establishment offering nude entertainment. All of the strip clubs in Cook County were BYOB.

"Keep your fucking mouth shut," I said. "Don't ruin the surprise for Evie."

The black door swung open and both the music and the roar of people got louder. I shuffled through, the future Mr. and Mrs. Stone trailing right behind. Dominic and I scanned the large, open room, and he pointed across the way.

"There."

An open table waited near the stage. He hurried to claim it while I led the blind slowly through the crowded area, trying to keep Logan from tripping over chair legs. I ignored the looks of the other patrons who probably wondered what the hell we were doing.

"Can I take it off?" Logan said loudly over the music.

"I don't think this is the right crowd for that."

Did he just growl at me? "The blindfold, Payton."

"Not yet." I put my hands on his shoulders and shoved him down into a chair, then helped Evie to hers.

Dominic twisted the cap off the whiskey. "Evie, you want champagne? Or rum and Coke?"

I reached for the unopened bottle. "It's Evelyn, and she'll take a rum and Diet Coke."

Dominic smirked. "You're so bossy."

"You love it." We happened to arrive at the perfect moment, right as the last performer was exiting, so we had a moment of quiet. "Okay, blindfolds off. Time to look at some real women."

The deejay's voice blared over the music, announcing a new dancer coming to the stage as Evie pulled off her mask. I'd been nice enough to let her leave her crown in the back of the limo. Her eyes went totally white, they were that wide open. She gazed at the dim room, draped in garish red velvet curtains and mirrors, and the large stage with gold poles. Around us, the other club goers were curious.

Evie and I were the only dressed women in the packed audience.

The room felt smoky, although smoking wasn't allowed and I didn't see a fog machine running. It was a haze of sex and seediness. I hadn't felt this kind of dirty on me since my blindfold club days, and I'd missed it, just a little.

"Holy shit, I'm in a strip club," Evie said.

Dominic flagged over one of the servers. "You haven't been before?"

She shook her head slowly, her gaze locked on the woman who sashayed over, a round tray tucked under one arm. The waitress's other hand rested on her hip, barely covered by black hot pants. The piercing in her navel winked under a strobe light. Her hot pink halter top was more like a bra than a shirt, and the padding beneath pushed her boobs together, giving her a great deal of cleavage.

Her tips were probably killer; she was hot. I wondered if I should snap a picture and send it to Joseph. He'd trolled strip clubs in the past when he was first getting started, but he'd never found a girl who was seriously interested in the job, was drug-free, and reliable. Most of his newer girls came from referrals now.

"Hi!" the waitress said with a wide smile, her hand touching Dominic's arm. "What can I get for you, hon?"

My annoyance flared, but I stayed quiet while he ordered the Diet Coke, plus some glasses and an ice bucket for the table. On stage, a lanky blonde in a black bra and fuchsia G-string was strutting in her stripper shoes. I admired the tattoos running along her rib cage. On the right girl and in the right setting, ink was hot.

"How does she dance in those?" Evie whispered to me.

The sole of the shoe was black, but the seven-inch heel and tall platform base were both a matching fuchsia, which glowed under the black light. The straps over the top of her foot were clear acrylic.

I shrugged at Evie's question. "Practice."

They didn't seem to give the blonde any trouble. She swayed with the sexy song pouring from the speakers, her lower body undulating to the rhythm. Her hands caressed her curves, teasing the removal. Fingers dipped below the G-string band at her hips, pulling it away for a second, only to return it into position, saving it for the big finish later.

I adjusted in my chair, setting a hand on Dominic's thigh, and his fingers curled over mine, holding my hand in place. Did he do this simply because he wanted to hold my hand? Or was he worried I would migrate further north to his cock? God, he knew me so well.

The stripper reached to set a hand high on the pole, wrapped her legs around it, and up she went. When she'd climbed to the top, her legs went straight out, parallel to the floor, and one knee bent, crossing over on top of the other leg. Her hands let go and she tipped back until she was upside-down, the pole clamped tight between her thighs. As she swung, her blonde hair fluttered behind.

There were murmurs of approval from the audience watching, and it built into a roar when her hands disappeared behind her back, and the bra was flung to the back of the stage.

"Holy shit!" Evie gasped and Logan chuckled.

The acrobatic work was impressive, and obviously I wasn't the only one who thought so. Guys lined up to throw crumbled dollar bills on the stage while she worked the pole. Her graceful moves, toned body, and tight breasts were sexy as hell.

"You're going to tip the stripper?" Evie asked when Logan dug out his wallet.

"No, naughty girl. You are."

I heard her hard swallow over the thump of the music. On stage, the stripper descended the spinning pole and planted her shoes back on the ground. She turned, bent over, and shoved her ass at the crowd, shimmying. More roars and cheers when she teased removing the tiny scrap of underwear once again.

This time she did it, exposing her bare pussy for everyone to see. Dominic's grip on my hand tightened subtly, then relaxed. "Fuck, she's hot."

I grinned. Did he know how much I loved hearing him say that? He was confident enough to know this wouldn't bother me. He was a man, hardwired to be attracted to tits and ass, and it seemed fucking stupid for him to hide it. Let him look and enjoy. I was. And my tits and ass were nicer, not to mention Dominic owned every inch of me, which made my ass a million times better.

Evie snatched the five-dollar bill from Logan and stood swiftly. She charged toward the end of the line of men waiting to tip, her face determined.

"That was . . . unexpected." Logan's expression had an edge of concern. Maybe he'd expected her to be too shy.

Like blood in the water, the men noticed her presence as a herd, and a few jaws dropped open. They parted, all gesturing for her to go to the front of the line. "Hey, ladies first," one of them said.

Evie was probably bright red. I couldn't see with her back facing us, but one of the guys at the front leaned over and said something close to her ear. She turned to look up at him wide-eyed, and Logan bolted out of his chair.

"Wait," Dominic called. "It's cool."

Apparently all the man had said to Evie was to put the money on her lips, which she did. *Yeah, Evie.* I laughed as the fully nude blonde took one look at my friend with a five-dollar bill on her face, and sauntered her direction. I had to believe every pair of eyes in the building were watching as the stripper palmed her breasts, and leaned into Evie so she was nuzzled between them.

"Fuck," Logan swore in appreciation. "I think I have another five."

The blonde's breasts were pushed together, so when

the stripper stepped back, the five-dollar bill was stuck in her cleavage. People hollered for her to do it again, and someone yelled for Evie to take her top off. That sobered Logan quickly.

"Save your money," Dominic said. "We've got a private room we can head to whenever you want."

Logan's attention turned to Dominic, stunned and yet grateful, and it was clear he understood. A private room meant lap dances away from an unwanted audience. Right now there were dances going on in the open booths lining the left wall. Anyone could watch the girls as they slid their bodies over the customers, which was sexy, and also safer for the dancers. But the strippers always had bras and panties on. We'd get to see more in the private room.

Sure enough, Evie's face was flamingly red when she turned on her heel and marched back toward our table, but she held her chin up. As she made her way through the tables of men, they stared up at her, lust in their eyes, and it was clear that wasn't lost on her. Oh, there was power in being a desired woman. I knew about that. At times, the power could be downright addictive.

"Did you enjoy yourself?" Logan asked, his lips teasing a smile.

"Did you, boss?" Her voice was casual. "She smelled like strawberries."

The server came by with our glasses, and Dominic doled them out to the table. We drank and watched a few more performers, but no one held a candle to that first blonde who'd mastered the pole.

The shower show was nice. The ebony stripper had fantastic tits, and they looked even better when they were glossed with soap and water. As we finished our drinks, a redhead wandered past, dragging her hand along my shoulders.

"Do you or any of your friends want a dance?"

"Maybe in a little bit," Dominic answered for me. She smiled and flitted away, and he turned quickly to me. "Unless you were into her? Did I just make a horrible mistake?"

"Please. You know I've got my eye on someone else."

We hadn't talked about me getting a lap dance, he just knew. His eyes lit with amusement. "The blonde?"

I nodded as my hand tried to travel a line up to his dick, but he squeezed my wrist. "Control yourself." His expression went strict and hard. "Or I'll do it for you."

Evil, evil man. Saying that in his dark voice turned the volume up on my lust until it was deafening. Yet, he had a good reason to stop me. I'd feel awful if I got us kicked out and Evie and Logan's night came to an abrupt end.

"What do you think?" Logan said to Dominic, nodding toward the glowing neon sign that announced the private rooms.

"Let's do it." Dominic gathered up our supplies and the ice bucket holding the champagne.

"We're leaving?" Evie sucked in a breath, probably horrified at how disappointed that had come out sounding.

"No, Evie," Dominic said. "I'm gonna buy Logan a lap dance. You get to pick out the girl."

The future Mr. and Mrs. Stone exchanged a glance.

Choose wisely, Evie. I needed him to beg for sex so we could both win our little competitions.

Logan's intense eyes stared down at her. "You should do the lap dance. You're the hottest girl in here."

Dominic cleared his throat, but Logan remained unfazed. Thankfully Evie didn't fall for it, and she scanned the room, evaluating the girls working the floor. Her focus settled on a leggy brunette with shoulder-length hair and a pretty face, and sexy librarian glasses that were probably just for show. Yet they made her look cute and studious, which would definitely appeal to anal-retentive Logan.

"Her," Evie said. Her smug voice matched her expression, saying she was confident in this decision.

We went to the bouncer waiting beside the doorway, and I pointed out who we wanted to come join us in our private party. He nodded, wrote it down on a clipboard, and told us we were in room three.

The narrow hallway was dimly lit and bare bones, and there were a total of three rooms judging by the numbers on the door. I opened ours and was pleasantly surprised. It had a large tufted couch in red and two black chairs opposite it, with a low table in the center for our drinks. In the corner, a lit platform surrounded a pole. The hallway had been kind of gross, but this was nice.

Dominic and I each took a chair as Logan sat on the couch. "Come here," he said to his fiancé. "Are you okay with this?"

She let out a short laugh. "Me? Yeah."

It did seem silly to ask, given what we'd done, but at

the same time I appreciated how important Evie's level of comfort was to him. He always did his best not to fuck up with her again.

"Let's establish rules," Logan said.

Evie gave him a dubious look. "You want more rules?"

"Guidelines," he amended. "I'm allowed to touch you. Kiss you. Everything except for sex is fair game."

Evie bit down on her lip and shook her head. "Part of the rule is no nudity—"

"As long as I don't violate that."

She didn't get a chance to answer him, for a sharp knock came from the door, and it swung open a half-second later. The leggy brunette with glasses. She was even cuter up close. *Good.*

She gave a shy smile, undoubtedly part of her act. "I'm Tracy. Someone wanted a dance?"

Dominic pointed out Logan. "He's getting married next weekend."

Tracy made the appropriate small talk that was probably club required, congratulating Logan. Thankfully, I didn't have to do that when I'd been seeing clients at the blindfold club, because I fucking sucked at talking.

The garter around Tracy's thigh was holding a lot of twenties, and I wondered how much she made a night. Nowhere near as much as I did at the blindfold club I was sure, but she also made hers legally. She fidgeted with her lacy red bra and matching panties, as if anxious to get them off. Her curves were nice. Big breasts, and a round ass that begged to be touched.

"You sure you're okay with this, sweetheart?" Tracy asked Evie. I'd stopped listening to the conversation for a moment, she must have figured out the bride was right beside the groom.

Evie gave a devious smile and nodded.

"Okay," she said to Logan. "Can you open your knees? I need some room."

When Logan leaned back against the couch and relaxed his legs, Tracy put one knee between them, sliding it up and down, right over the fly of his pants. Her hands twisted behind her back and undid the clasp of her bra, and she held the cups to her chest for a moment before dropping the fabric away.

Her tits were immediately in his face.

Evie's breathing picked up as she watched the topless woman grind on her soon-to-be husband, but she didn't look anxious. Nope, she was getting turned on. She crossed her legs and put her hands together in her lap, almost as if she wanted to touch Logan but didn't want to get in the stripper's way.

Tracy's hands fondled her breasts, massaging them as she slid up and down his face. The music from the main stage was pumped into the VIP room and wafted from a speaker in the corner. She moved in time with the song that was all about fucking, letting her body give us a perfect visual.

When she straddled Logan's lap and rode him, everyone else in the room froze. Were they as unprepared as I was for how hot the scene was? Logan's hands splayed on her thighs around him, just resting there. Tracy didn't seem to mind.

"Fuck, Evie, kiss me."

A startled smile broke on her face. "Yeah? Are you having a *hard* time?"

"He's getting there," Tracy said, flashing a wink. Then she rose up on her knees, undulating while her hands ran up and down his chest, caressing him through his dress shirt.

I flinched when Dominic's fingers skimmed my knee. I'd been so engrossed watching the show I hadn't noticed he'd pulled his chair closer to mine. I leaned in and breathed in his ear, my words barely a whisper.

"I want to fuck you so bad right now."

"I know." He gave me a triumphant smile.

This was Dominic when he was most in control, and he loved his power. There'd been so many nights when we'd played with Akira and Yuriko, and I'd been writhing under his command, desperate to hold it together and begging for him to fuck me. He'd spent the first few months following Akira's lead when to reward, but his confidence had grown to no longer need advice. Dominic knew exactly when to give me what I craved, and how long to deny it to maximize our pleasure. Or make me crazy. Sometimes they were the same.

Tracy's hand flowed down the line of buttons on the front of Logan's shirt, over his belt, and . . .

"Shit." Logan groaned it through clenched teeth.

I raised an eyebrow at Dominic. Was that sort of

thing allowed? Dominic shrugged.

"You're barely looking at her," Evie said to him. "Don't you think she's hot?"

I cut the chuckle off before it slipped out. She was taunting him, trying to win her bet, and I fucking loved it. Plus, she was right. It seemed as if Logan was struggling and avoiding the scene as much as possible.

He groaned, low and frustrated. His hand hooked around the nape of Evie's neck and dragged her across the couch so he could crush his lips to hers while the stripper raked her fingernails over his zipper. I drew a deep breath in, sipping the air that was heavy with desire.

Tracy stood while Logan continued to deliver a passionate kiss, his mouth moving over Evie's with reckless abandon. Tracy turned and sat in his lap, rubbing her ass against the bulge of Logan's cock. Her creamy tits jiggled with her movements, and I fought to keep still. I wanted to touch her, or for Dominic to touch me, or both. My skin was tight with lust and I needed relief.

Evie moaned when Logan's hand trailed down her neck, over her collarbone, and settled on her breast. It was then that Tracy leaned to put her back against Logan's chest, her head resting on his shoulder opposite Evie. The dancer continued to squirm, and her movements were obviously having an impact on him.

Her head turned toward him, and I caught a flash of Tracy's tongue as it dipped out to lick the side of Logan's neck. He jerked and his free hand wrapped around her hip.

"Look at him," I whispered to Dominic. "Living the

fucking dream."

He smiled back like the devil.

Behind the gyrating body, Logan fought for breath, or maybe to maintain his control. To go more than a month without sex, to kissing Evie while a nearly naked stripper humped him . . .

"Someone's a lucky girl," Tracy said, glancing at Evie. "His dick is huge."

Evie's face colored a shade of pink, and that was her only response. But the blush quickly faded when Tracy stood and swayed to the music, her fingers creeping beneath the band of lace at her hips. She rocked her thumbs down painfully slow, one side then the other, as her underwear began its taunting descent.

There was a sharp inhale from Evie when the red panties were lowered to mid-thigh, just below the money-filled garter. Tracy bent forward and set her warm hands on my knees. Her ass wiggled, shoving her bare pussy right in Logan's face. All the while she smiled at me behind her glasses.

"You're pretty fucking hot," I said.

She tossed her hair over a shoulder, and for a split second I wondered if she was bashful, but she laughed softly. "Thanks, girl."

"You never answered me," Logan said, his voice hurried.

Evie's gaze seemed unable to leave Tracy's hypnotizing pussy. "About?"

"The guidelines, naughty girl. I need to know . . .

what's allowed."

The dancer's ankles came together. She stood straight, arched her back, and the panties fell to a heap at her feet. Holy fuck, she looked good in nothing but her money, glasses, and high heels. Dominic and I didn't get to look at the long, nude curve of her body for more than a few seconds. She turned to face the couch and knelt between Logan's knees while her hands ran along his inseam, working her way up.

"Fucking shit." Logan combed his fingers through his hair and tipped his head back on the couch. Evie was sucking on his neck. Tracy's hands unbuckled his belt. His pants were unsnapped and a zipper dropped. *Oh my God.*

It wasn't clear if Logan was trying to sit up and stop Tracy, or if he was moving to make it easier. By the time he was sitting upright, the fully naked woman dropped down into his lap, right over his erection covered by a thin layered of black cotton.

"Shit. Shit, wait a minute," he said. His hands were on her undulating hips in an attempt to stop her. His eyes were hooded with lust, but still focused on Evie. But this didn't seem to bother his fiancé.

"Does she feel good?" Evie's smile was diabolical, and pride burned warm in my veins. It was exciting to see this side of her, the one who was powerful. It had come out for a moment in Logan's darkened bedroom that night last September when she'd let me join them. She'd pushed Logan right to the edge. Her voice was as commanding now as it had been then. "Tell me how bad you want me."

"Goddamnit."

"Tell me," Evie goaded, "what you want to do to me."

Tracy slithered over his cock, her pussy grinding against him. Were his eyes going to roll back into his head? He looked a half-second away from tossing Tracy away, slamming Evie into the couch, pushing her panties aside, and taking her in one, quick thrust.

He seemed like he might give up with his next breath.

"I want you to ride my fingers." He was panting now. His face had an intense, raw expression. "I want you coming on my face. Now, fucking tell me . . . is that allowed?"

"You'll violate the nudity—"

"No, naughty girl." He gave her a frantic kiss, as if he only had a fingertip's grip on his control. "Payton has blindfolds."

Of course. Kind of cheating, but not. *Clever, Logan.*

Chapter FIVE

Evie's blue eyes blinked at his question, and it was so clear. She wanted to say yes desperately, but also feared what giving him that power would do. I feared it as well. Men were most persuasive when they were on their knees.

"Answer me." It was a whisper from Logan, but his demanding tone made it sound loud.

"Yes," Evie said breathlessly. "But if you peek, I win."

Logan's smile was a million miles wide. "That won't happen, but I get it."

Tracy picked up the pace, sliding faster on him and the muscles along Logan's jawline flexed. He looked like he was enduring punishment.

The pads of Dominic's fingers traced circles on my knee and threatened to venture up onto my inner thigh. My legs parted slightly to make room and encourage, but he didn't take the bait. He just sat there, tracing his infuriating and teasing circles while I ached for his touch.

The song faded out and was replaced by another, and the waves of Tracy's hips slowed to a stop. "You want another dance, sexy?"

"No, thank you." It was tight and relieved from Logan.

Oh, hell no. He'd survived the lap dance, but I sensed he was wound tighter than a spring. Maybe he just needed another push.

"She wants a dance," I said, gesturing to Evie. "My treat."

The noise of protest that escaped Logan sounded suspiciously nervous, as Tracy lifted onto her knees and began crawling into Evie's lap. Who went statue-still with shock.

"You can touch me," Tracy whispered, her voice warm like honey. "Forget about club rules, I don't mind." Her knees were planted on either side of Evie's lap, and her hands tousled her light brown hair. Then her palms flowed down her neck, over her bare breasts, tweaking her nipples to keep them hard. Or maybe she simply enjoyed the sensation.

Tracy finished wandering her own body, and traveled over to the front of Evie's dress. Her fingers dipped inside the neckline. Evie's mouth fell open but no sound came out.

The woman glanced at Logan. "Is she shy?"

I snorted. "Only with strangers."

"Oh, shit." Evie's shoulders shuddered when Tracy latched her lips on Evie's neck. Hands moved under the neckline of her dress.

Dominic gripped my knee and tugged, drawing my focus to him. His dark, seductive look made my breath hitch. Lust hung heavy in the air, choked my lungs, and I was snared in his gaze.

"Get the fuck over here. You're too far away," he said in his rough, deep voice.

Too far away for him to undoubtedly torture me, but I went to him anyway, eager. I scrambled to sit sideways in his lap. His hold tangled in my hair and yanked me down into his kiss while his other hand slid up my leg, diving beneath my skirt.

Fuck yes.

I could hear movement on the couch that sounded as if Logan was doing up his pants. Did he have blue balls, aching to be inside his fiancé? Because I could fucking relate. Whatever the female equivalent of that was, I had it. I *needed* Dominic. Somehow the restraint Evie had placed on Logan had an effect on me. It was like how denial instantly intensifies a craving.

Dominic feathered the lightest touch over my panties, but it was a bolt of static electricity on my sensitized skin.

"Yes," I whispered. "More."

His lips hovered by the shell of my ear. "Where?" His fingers brushed again. "Here?"

"Yes," I hissed. I gripped his forearm and squeezed. I both hated and loved his teasing.

"But you didn't say please, Payton."

"Fuck." I squirmed to try to get his fingers against me. I was soaking through the lace, and now I wished he hadn't given me permission to wear the underwear. The barrier between us needed to go, but Dominic held me firm.

Logan's voice cut through the fog, spoken with pride. "Naughty girl."

Holy shit. Evie had a hand on Tracy's tits, and her big, blue eyes stared up at the naked woman writhing in her lap. There was a tiny, unexpected spark of jealousy at this, which was ridiculous. I was the last woman Evie had been with. She and Logan hadn't invited anyone else to play after me, or so she said. I loved my best friend, but not in that way, and I'd gone on to play with other women, so wasn't I a fucking hypocrite?

"Is this okay?" she whispered to Logan.

His hand pushed down his erection, adjusting in his seat. "Are you serious? It's so fucking hot." He leaned in and swallowed her moan as he kissed her.

Dominic pressed a finger right to my clit, and I jolted. "Eyes on me, devil woman."

"Yes, Sir." I'd meant it to sound sarcastic, but this man made me fall apart. His expression was full of power and control as he stroked me. His fingers toyed with the seam, mocking that he'd move the fabric to the side and *really* touch me.

Speaking of mocking . . .

"Did you need something?" Evie said. I didn't dare take my eyes off Dominic, but I could hear the confidence in her voice. "You look like you need something."

"I'm fine, Evie." It would have been more believable if Logan's voice hadn't sounded uneven. "But watching you suck on her tits has me so fucking hard."

"What? I haven't done that."

"You're about to."

Evie blew out a breath. It was quiet, and then Tracy's low moan rang out. I wanted to watch what was happening. I was turned away to face Dominic, but he could see it all, and since I was in his lap, I felt the subtle jerk of his cock against my thigh.

His gaze flicked up to meet mine, and an indecent

smile crept over him. "Your friend's licking the stripper's tits."

Why was I surprised that she'd done it? Obviously she didn't have a problem with women, and Logan had basically told her to. The good girl loved following his commands. But I was thrilled, too. This had been strategic on Evie's part, I was sure. She'd do what she could to win.

"And what about your friend? Does he look ready to break a rule?"

Even without seeing him, I could feel Logan's gaze boring into me. "No, he doesn't," he answered for Dominic.

But since I had obeyed my fiancé, he rewarded me. My breath evaporated in a shiver when my panties were tugged to the side and a finger plunged inside. My fingernails dug into his forearm at the welcomed intrusion.

"Slow," the rough voice echoed in my ear, just a whisper. "Don't rush me, or I'll stop. You don't want that, do you?"

I shook my head and clamped my teeth together to choke back the plea for *more*, and *faster*, and *harder*. God, all of what he'd give me, if only I had patience. Pleasure grew in slow waves, building with Dominic's painstakingly slow pace, and the thumb that teased my clit.

A soft moan slipped from my lips. If he expected me to be quiet, he was going to have to tell me.

"Ready to start revising the rule?" Logan's tone was wicked. "If I put my hand up your skirt, am I going to find your pussy wet and ready for me?"

Evie gasped. "Oh my God."

"That's not an answer."

Dominic's mouth captured mine, and his tongue slid past my lips. It possessed and tasted, and I returned the kiss with the same intensity he fed me. My next moan was louder, and two fingers delved into my greedy body. The stretch was delicious, but wasn't enough. His skilled fingers were amazing, but I hungered for the real thing.

Time began to blur. It was burned up by the heat Dominic was injecting me with. Abruptly the fingers retreated and I whined, but Dominic shushed me. He *fucking shushed* me—

The wet fingers were shoved in my mouth, cutting me off. I sucked them clean, and it was then I realized why. Tracy stood in front of us, her bra and panties back on, and an expectant look.

"It's eighty," she said softly.

Dominic pulled out his wallet and pushed the Yen aside, digging out the American money. He counted out five twenty-dollar bills and handed them over. "Thanks."

"Thank you." She winked, thrilled with the tip. "Can I get you guys anything?"

"Yeah. There was a blonde on the main stage when we got here—"

"The one with the amazing pole skills," I interrupted.

Tracy slipped the twenties into her garter. "Ashley. I'll see if she's available to party with you."

As soon as she was out the door, Dominic reached for his glass of whiskey, and he chuckled right before tipping the glass back. It was because Evie had hurled herself into

Logan's lap and his hand disappeared under her skirt.

"You can tell me you don't want to fuck," Logan said, "but your body says otherwise."

Evie sighed and clung to him. "You know I want to. This is all your fault."

"How's that?"

"You're the one with all the rules and who loves anticipation."

His expression was skeptical. Clearly he didn't believe her.

"Green . . ." She kissed his lips. "Yellow." She rocked her hips on him. "Red." Her hand gripped his cock through his pants. "You've taught me all about the build-up, boss."

Logan looked smug. His dark eyes studied her as he continued to move his hand between her legs.

"You let me know . . ." she said in a tight voice, "when you think you're so persuasive that I'm going to cave."

His short laugh was full of confidence. "I'll let you know when I start, but here's a clue. I'll have a blindfold on."

Evie's expression shifted into one of fear. "Wait, I've changed my mind. You can't go down on me."

Logan hesitated. "What?"

"No oral. Well, I can still go down on you—"

Oh, he did *not* like hearing that. His expression hardened. "Bullshit. You already set the rules, you can't go back on them."

His arm flexed and moved, as if he'd thrust his finger deep inside her. Evie inhaled sharply and balled his shirt into her fists.

"Fuck," she cried, twisting with pleasure and pain.

"No changing the rules during the game, naughty girl. Understood?"

It was barely a word from her. "Yes." It was immediately followed by a moan and she melted into Logan's embrace.

The door swung open without a knock, and in strolled the blonde on her black and fuchsia shoes. She was even better looking up close, but there was a cold, ruthless look in her eyes that I was a little too familiar with. This had been me at the blindfold club. Disconnected. Doing the job while being numb.

Ashley didn't have the people skills Tracy did—she was all business. "It's fifty for a two song dance. Forty for one song if you want me on the pole."

"Fifty," Dominic said. "My fiancé wants a dance."

She gave a plain look. "Sorry, I don't do women."

I . . . couldn't even. She took the money from Evie's lips earlier without a problem. I found the girl's rejection annoying, even though it wasn't personal. She had every right to refuse, but . . . "You don't like money?"

Ashley's face soured, and when she wasn't smiling, she had a full-on case of resting bitch face. "I do, but I'm not into girls."

Her condescending tone was sharp as a knife, slicing both Evie and I, but she didn't appear concerned about it. Her gaze flitted from Dominic to Logan, and her whole demeanor changed. Her face lit up and her voice warmed like honey. "Do either of you guys want a dance?"

This girl made her living dancing for men, and she was a seasoned pro. One who assumed either Logan or Dominic held the money, and she'd have more luck getting extra dances out of the guy with the wallet if he was the one receiving.

"No, they don't want a dance." I snatched my drink off the table and slammed it. "But thanks for stopping by."

Her eyes widened with surprise. Surely she was used to being the most powerful woman in the room, but then, she'd never been in one with *me*.

"I can get on the pole for thirty." Like she was sensing the sale slipping away.

I gestured to Dominic. "You know what? He'll take a lap dance after all . . . for thirty."

Her eyes went narrow, but she didn't walk. How confident was she in her skills in getting more dances out of him? Apparently confident enough. She nodded in reluctant acceptance and strutted toward us.

Alcohol buzzed in my system, but when I rose to stand on my sexy high heels, I tried not to show the effects. I rounded the chair so I could set my hands on Dominic's shoulders and lean over. It wasn't my first choice, but I liked this. It was a position of power and a front row seat to the dance.

Ashley's gaze paused on mine, and she issued a silent threat to keep my distance. *Whatever, bitch.* I'd touch him if I wanted to. Dominic would throw her ass to the ground if I asked him to do it.

The song changed and Ashley began her dance. Her

feet moved side to side on those sexy heels while her hands wandered over her body. It felt . . . forced and robotic. Not alluring and seductive like Tracy's had been. Dammit, why didn't I just ask her to stay? Every second Ashley looked less and less attractive to me.

Her bra came off quickly and was cast to the floor as she remained on her feet, swaying to the music. Her hands stacked her blonde hair up on top of her head, and then it fell, cascading down as she shook her head, her tits bouncing slightly.

She spun on her heels and flopped down, putting her ass in Dominic's lap so she could grind on him. Would he even find this sexy? I felt bad for agreeing to the dance without checking with him first. I needed to make this better. *Hotter.*

I bent down and settled my lips a breath away from Dominic's, teasing my kiss. I even lowered until our lips barely touched, but didn't give him the pressure and intensity I knew he desired. His hand shot up, grabbed a handful of hair on the back of my head and forced me down so our mouths could crash together, while the other woman rocked in his lap.

But the impact of our kiss made my drunk ass stumble on my heels. *Shit!* My hand latched onto anything to stabilize and keep me from falling. I found something soft, and warm, and bare.

Ashley's shoulder.

I yanked my hand back and straightened, but she jolted up out of his lap and spun to face me, anger flaring in her eyes.

"That was my bad," Dominic said. Ashley snatched up her discarded bra, not bothering to put it back on. "She didn't mean to—"

But Ashley fled without a word, exited the room in a huff, and the door slammed shut.

I blinked at Evie and Logan who were frozen on the couch, staring back at me, and since I was drunk, I no longer cared about my filter. She'd run from the room just because I accidentally touched her shoulder? "God, what a lesbian."

Dominic chuckled.

"You know what?" I said. "I think Tracy's hotter anyway, I'm sure we can get—"

The door opened and a thick white guy with no neck stepped inside, a sneer on his face. "Party's over. Time to go."

Chapter SIX

My mouth dropped open. "Are you fucking serious?"

The bouncer surveyed the room and his gaze landed on Dominic. "Yeah, you can't touch the dancers. You all need to leave."

"He didn't touch her," I said. "I did, and it was completely on accident."

The enormous man shook his head and crossed his powerful arms over his chest. "Not what the girl said, but it doesn't matter."

"This is bullshit."

"Are we going to have a problem here?"

Dominic's hands were on my waist, locking me in place, as if he knew I was a heartbeat away from getting in the bouncer's face. I drew in a breath to even myself out and remain in control. It was done, and no amount of talking was going to salvage it. "Nope, no problem." I put my hand on top of Dominic's, urging him to release me. "Let's go. I'm fucking exhausted anyway. The jet lag is catching up."

It wasn't possible to feel worse than I did as we were escorted through the club toward the main door. There were round tables near the entrance that had poles in the center so the dancers could entertain smaller parties, up close and personal. Ashley, back in her bra, was up on the table, dancing for a group of men.

I felt a little better when several of the guys turned my direction and watched me. From the annoyed expression on her face, I could tell she knew. These men preferred to look at me, fully clothed, over her in a bra and skimpy underwear.

The night air was cool as we waited for Saul to pull the limo up.

"Guys," I said. "I'm sorry."

Evie shivered in the breeze, but laughed. "It wasn't your fault. And think about how awesome the story is. I got kicked out of a strip club during my bachelorette party."

Logan's hands rubbed up and down her arms, trying to warm her. "Payton, it's not a problem."

"Of course not. You're just dying to get your blindfold back on."

Logan's grin developed slowly, and it looked seductive and sinister in the moonlight, much like a predator's, and Evie was his prey. "You're not wrong."

The limo pulled up and Saul hopped out, opening the back door. Evie and Logan climbed inside, but I motioned for Dominic to go next, and set a hand on our driver's arm.

"Can you just drive around for the next forty-five minutes or so? Stay in the city, but keep us moving?"

If it was an odd request, Saul didn't show it. "Sure, not a problem."

"Thanks." As I climbed in and shut the door, I wondered how much of our party he could hear behind the black privacy glass. Maybe he'd go home tonight and tell his wife about chauffeuring us from drag queen club to titty bar, or perhaps this wasn't that wild of a night for him. He was a limo driver in Chicago and might have driven all sorts of crazy celebrities.

"No more liquor for you." I tugged the champagne glass from Evie's hand. I didn't want it to be any easier on Logan. In fact, I wanted him to need a crowbar to get her knees apart.

"What's going on?" The corners of her mouth turned downward. "Earlier you acted like you thought I was insane, and now you're on board?"

"Yeah," Dominic said before I could get anything out. "Now that she's got something riding on it."

Logan held an amused smile. "You made a bet?" His gaze settled on mine. "You're going to lose."

Dominic laughed. "I told her that."

Cocky pieces of shit, both of them. "Hey, fuck you. You both think you're so irresistible, why don't you try to seduce each other?" I sipped the drink I'd stolen from Evie as the limo took a turn and forced me to lean into Dominic. I set my hand on his chest and pushed off, righting myself. "Evie and I could watch."

It was like I'd insulted their mothers. Both men gave me an annoyed look, illustrating exactly how *not funny* that idea was to them.

"You're a bunch of hypocrites," I continued. "You love girl-on-girl, but you don't give us any guy-on-guy action."

Evie giggled at the thought. Shit. She sounded like I felt. Buzzing.

"Keep dreaming, devil woman."

I made a pouty face, but then I got an idea. The drink sloshed as I abandoned it in a cup holder and set my sights on Evie. She was sitting on the side bench, closest to the front of the limo, which meant I'd have to climb over Logan to get to her.

Strong arms ensnared me as I tried to move, and his low voice rumbled in my ear. "And where do you think you're going?"

"To get some girl-on-girl action," I whispered back, "since I didn't get any at the club." Instantly Dominic's hold was gone.

Logan eyed me with suspicion as I fumbled through the aisle. The car hit a bump and I tumbled into his lap.

"Don't mind me," I said, full of sarcasm. Which of course, he didn't. Logan made zero effort to help me, but perhaps he wanted to keep his distance. Dominic and I hadn't talked much about the fact I'd fucked his best friend, because it had happened months before I'd met the man who became my fiancé. But tension lurked in the quiet moments, and Logan didn't seem to know how to deal. It needed to not be so quiet.

"Get out your phone and put on some music," I ordered Logan. "Something sexy."

He didn't move. "What exactly is your plan?"

I flopped down on the seat between the bride and groom, edging Evie out of the way. "Evie's going to give me a lap dance."

Her laugh was bright and bubbly. She thought I was

kidding? Because I wasn't.

The dark back seat glowed with soft light when Logan began tapping on his screen, and then a slow, seductive beat began.

"Come on," I said to her, my voice going husky. "Let's see if we can get Logan to come in his pants." How would Evie beg him for sex if he were already spent?

Logan's tone was dark. "You're hilarious. That won't happen, so there's no need to try."

"Logan," Dominic barked. "Shut the fuck up."

I grinned. Dominic hadn't gotten to see Evie and me together, after all. It was only fair.

"Okay." She flashed a smile as she shook her head. "Get ready for the least sexy lap dance ever."

I'd cut her some slack. She was a little drunk. Even though the limo was spacious, it was still the interior of a car and didn't leave much room. Plus, it was in motion and she had an audience.

But when she sat down on my lap and stared at me, like that was all she had, I laughed. "Yeah, don't quit your day job."

"Yes, please don't," Logan quipped.

Evie leaned over and put a hand on his leg to stabilize herself. "I wouldn't dream of it, boss."

I hadn't lied at the club; I was exhausted. So I needed to get the show going if I had any hope of getting Logan turned on enough to ask her to break her rule. My palm slid up her spine, and I buried my fingers in her soft, thick hair, only to clench a fistful and tug her head back. A startled noise erupted from her when I planted my lips on the side of her throat, right where her pulse pounded.

Both men straightened, and the mood in the back seat snapped from playful to serious in an instant. My other hand cupped the side of her face, holding her still as I sucked on her neck, and her heartbeat raced.

"Oh." It escaped from Evie on the lightest of sighs.

She smelled like citrus. The tip of my nose traced her delicate skin, and I exhaled. It drew a shiver from her, and power rose in my belly. I'd learned how much I liked being in control the first night Akira let me have it over his submissive Yuriko. Dominic wouldn't have an issue now, but how much control would Logan let me take?

Without releasing my hold, I softened my grip on the hair at the nape of her neck, giving her just enough leash so she could see both men gazing at us. Their lustful expressions only fed my power.

"Can I touch her?" I asked Logan, knowing his response would dictate what kind of response I got from her. If he were into it, she'd allow it. My hand not in her hair crept down to rest on her collarbone, and my fingers edged just inside the shoulder of her dress. Hinting exactly where I wanted to go.

"If it's okay with Evie."

It was a dangerous game I hadn't intended to play again, but I couldn't stop myself. The pads of my fingers glided over her smooth skin, traveling down the fabric of her dress until the round globe of her breast was in my hand.

She didn't stop me, thank God. Over the song playing on Logan's phone, I heard both men's breathing pick up.

"Shit," she mumbled. "What are we doing?" Only she arched her sexually starved body into my touch.

"Just having some fun." I squeezed and her nipple harden beneath her bra. *So responsive.* My mouth went back to her throat, and as I moved up, she turned her head down . . .

Our lips met. *She* kissed me.

Her warm, soft mouth tasted like champagne and sin, and her hands cupped my face. Passionate. Delicate fingers brushed my cheek, and abruptly she shifted in my lap. Moving so she could straddle my legs, and devote all of her attention to me. Did she have the same thought as I did?

Either way, it was thrilling. Once again her skirt was almost to her hips, giving a hint of the dark panties she wore beneath. The new position made it easier to touch her tits, which I did. Her full C-cup breasts were so different from Yuriko's.

Evie rocked in my lap, stirring her hips, and grinding against me to the beat of the music.

"So you do know how to give a lap dance." Both of my hands massaged her breasts, pushing them together. "I think you should take off your dress."

Her eyes grew big.

"Nice try," Logan said. "You've had your fun, Payton." A surprised noise choked in Evie's throat when Logan grabbed her around the waist and hauled her into his lap, his eyes glinting with determination. "Dominic, do you mind if we sit there?"

He didn't. As soon as Logan was gone, carrying Evie to the seat in the rear, Dominic took his seat beside me. The song faded out and another replaced it. This one was still sexy, but sounded dirtier. *Perfect.*

"I need the blindfolds." It was an order from Logan.

Wait, no. Shit, I was going to lose. Evie settled into the seat and pressed back into it, her hands spread on her thighs. Then she crossed her legs and looked just as nervous as I felt.

"I left them in the club," I lied.

He'd seen me put them away, but even if he hadn't, it wouldn't have mattered. Logan was like me and could read lies easily. "No, you didn't."

I gave Dominic a traitorous glare as he reached into my purse, produced the blindfolds, and passed them to his friend.

"Why don't you," Logan said to Dominic, "check the view out the window. See what's changed in the city since you've been gone."

"The windows are tinted and it's night out."

"Then stare at the fucking ceiling. Don't look back here."

I laughed. Logan was just as possessive as Dominic, maybe more. My guess was Logan was about to remove Evie's panties and he didn't want Dominic to see anything.

"Okay." Dominic exchanged a smirk with me. "I'll try."

When Logan moved in to kiss her, she looked wary. She took the blindfold, but didn't put it on. "I don't have to wear it. Seeing myself naked doesn't violate the rule."

Logan's expression was ruthless, and his tone was that of a dominant. "Put it on."

Fuck. It made me hot and my hand curled on Dominic's leg. Logan slid off the seat so he was kneeling on the floorboard, his back facing Dominic and me, and obscuring Evie from view just as she donned the black mask.

"No cheating," she said, her voice wavering.

Logan slipped the thin strap on the back of his head and positioned his blindfold down over his eyes. "I've got mine on now."

I hopped up into Dominic's lap, which allowed me to see over Logan's shoulder, and to put Dominic's hand on my thigh, high beneath my skirt. His warm palm smoothed up and down, but didn't move inward. No, not yet. He'd stoke the fire until I was desperate, and then he'd make me burn.

Evie flinched when Logan put his hands on her knees and urged her to uncross them. Her lips pressed together when his hands moved upward, carrying her skirt with it, all the way until her black panties were exposed. I barely got a look before Logan wrapped his fingers around the sides and began tugging them off.

"No sex," she said. Who exactly was she telling? It sounded more for herself than for him.

"No sex *with my cock*," he clarified.

I held my breath as the panties were worked past her knees, and she pulled one leg out, leaving the underwear on an ankle. A tiny landing strip of hair covered her slit, and it was sexy as hell. At her sides, Evie's hands were clenched into fists. Her chest heaved rapidly.

"How's that view, Dominic?" Logan asked.

"Still tinted and nighttime."

"Great." Logan's palms trailed up Evie's legs, gently pressing her knees apart. When he reached the juncture of her thighs, his hands curled, and he raked his fingernails down the insides of her legs, sensitizing her.

She jerked. "Oh my God."

Logan bent, lowering his mouth to her knee, and his lips glided along the faint pink track marks he'd left on her pale skin. Goosebumps lifted on her legs, and she shuddered as he closed in.

"I've been dying to lick this pussy for the last thirty-seven days, Evie."

Her tremble increased with anticipation as he hovered so close she could surely feel his breath. Her hands moved to clench the sides of her dress, and she went white-knuckled.

A short gasp punctuated the backseat when his mouth latched onto her clit. And since Logan was nestled between her parted legs, and they both had blindfolds on, there was no one to know Dominic was peeking except for me. I grinned and shook my head, but he just shrugged. Sort of like, *"Can you blame me?"* I couldn't. It was so fucking hot.

"Oh, shit," Evie said. Her back bowed from the leather seats, which forced Logan to clamp his hands on her legs, keeping her spread. Her head tilted back and she panted for breath as his tongue worked its way through her valley.

He didn't stop or slow when her hand crushed into his hair. Either trying to drive him back or hold him in place, I couldn't tell. Her moans grew louder as his face nuzzled. He attacked her like a man desperate for her orgasm, which he probably was. Maybe he'd edge her for a while and make her insane with need, just as Dominic loved to do to me. The tough skin of his palm caressed my thigh, each stroke inching closer to my pussy.

"God, don't stop." Evie's whisper was more of a plea.

My legs opened and I shoved Dominic's hand where I needed it, pressing his fingers to my aching clit. I shifted in his lap, rubbing myself against him. But it wasn't enough.

"You're not allowed to wear panties for the rest of the night." His dark voice was low and in my ear, too quiet for our friends to hear. *Yes.* I scrambled out of the underwear and shoved the wadded fabric in my purse, then pulled his hand right back to where it had been. It felt so fucking good when he touched me, just grazing my clit. My nerve endings sizzled and begged for more pressure.

Evie's legs were shaking. Her knees had gone lax and spread wide, her whole body under Logan's command. Only one hand was on her thigh. The other was beneath his mouth, working a finger inside her. It was slick with arousal, sliding in and out easily.

He paused. "You want another, naughty girl?"

She bit down on her bottom lip and nodded, but since he couldn't see, he continued to wait for an answer.

"Yes . . ." she said. "Oh!" Logan's first two fingers

eased inside.

"Goddamnit," Dominic whispered. "You're so wet. Maybe I should have left your panties on."

I shuddered when not one, but two fingers pushed inside me. Before I could moan loudly, his palm curled around my mouth.

"Quiet, Payton. Not a sound."

His warm lips feathered kisses on my neck, sending waves of delicious shivers through me. So I sat there and watched Evie ride Logan's fingers and tongue, while Dominic fucked me with two thick fingers, and struggled not to make a noise. I tried to contain the bliss that crashed into me and threatened to erupt. Dominic always found a way to put restraint on me, knowing how much I craved it. It made my release so much better.

My thumb rolled circles on his hard cock through his pants. How far would he allow me to go? Could I undo his belt and fuck him under my dress in front of our friends? They couldn't see, but they could certainly hear.

There was a cry of pleasure from Evie, and a soft pop as Logan pulled off suction from her pussy.

"Tell me you want my cock," he said as he straightened. His hands undid his pants. "Tell me how badly you need it."

Her face was half-covered with the blindfold, but it twisted with agony. "Oh, God, Logan . . ."

Dominic and I froze when Logan's boxers were tugged out of his way and his large dick was gripped in a hand. A nervous cry tore from Evie as he ran the tip of his cock through her wetness, testing her.

"Wait," she blurted out. Her hands flailed, finding his shoulders.

He pumped his hips, sliding up and down through her folds. My pussy clenched at the visual. I loved how that sensation felt, the ridge of Dominic's cock when he teased, skin on heated skin.

And holy shit. Was Logan going to break the rule?

He was right there. Only a slight push of his hips and he'd be inside her. Evie gulped down air like she was drowning. Her desire and his need were thick in the enclosed space, blanketing us all.

"Don't you want to?" Logan's words were coated in persuasion. Evil man. She squirmed beneath him. "Are you trying to get me to fuck you, naughty girl?"

Her expression flashed with guilt. "Please."

"Please, what?"

"Do it," she begged. "Just for a second."

Dominic's warm breath was at the shell of my ear. "I told you." *Dammit.*

Logan continued his slow, mocking thrusts while not sliding into her. "What about the rule?"

"I don't care anymore. You win, Logan. Fuck me, please."

"Shit, Evie. I *really* fucking want to . . ." His hands clenched on her waist, tightening to hold her still. "But I won't."

She gasped. "What? Why?"

"Because I love you. I'm not going to risk any regret

about tonight. What if we do this and you end up wishing we'd waited a few more days?" He reached a hand out, finding her face and guided himself to plant a kiss on her lips. "I promise I'll make it worth the wait."

Warmth spread through my chest, spiraling outward from my heart. Yeah, Logan was lucky to have Evie, but she was plenty lucky to have him, too. He always put her first, which to me was the definition of love.

I glanced at Dominic, who wore the same smile I probably had on my face. He'd give me whatever I needed, just as I'd do for him, no matter what.

"So," Logan said, "no sex until you make an honest man out of me. But I won't say no if you want to blow me right now."

She laughed and fused her lips to his. Their kiss was raw and powerful, and when she pulled back, she was grinning. But I knew her well. Beneath that blindfold, she was blinking back emotional tears. Her love for him was overwhelming.

"Where are you—" she said, but her words cut off as he bent back down. His tongue swirled where his cock had just been, and she twitched, like the pleasure had been intense. "Oh, shit."

He sank his fingers inside her, pumping them in a furious tempo, and his mouth rotated on her clit, hinting how much work was going beneath his lips. She bucked on the seat, groaning.

Her moans swelled with each passing second. "God, I'm close," she said. "I'm so fucking close."

It only made Logan increase his efforts. His hand not inside her body wandered up her stomach, grabbing a handful of her breast. That seemed to be the final straw to tip her over the edge.

"Fuck!" She seized as tremors tumbled down her legs. The muscles along her calves strained with the orgasm until she collapsed back against the seat with an enormous sigh. Her mouth was slack, and she panted for air.

Watching the ecstasy rip through her flipped a switch on Dominic. His fingers pulsed inside me, and teeth sank into the flesh of my earlobe, so his breath filled my ear. My mind couldn't focus on anything but this man. I groaned quietly into his rough palm that was covering my lips.

"Touch your pussy. Let's make this body come."

It was a command I was happy to follow. I buried my fingers in between my legs, rubbing the swollen nub, needing relief. God, his hands. The one fucking me was building my climax, but the one keeping me quiet was so dominating and hot.

Logan sat on the seat beside Evie, and she didn't waste any time switching positions with him. Her knees were on the floor, the panties still wrapped around an ankle, and her hands gripped his hard cock in the moment before it disappeared into her mouth.

It came on a low voice from Logan. "*Fuck.*"

Was there something wrong with me that I liked watching this? I enjoyed seeing her head bob on him, and loved listening to his heavy breathing. I was already unbearably turned on, but then Logan gathered her hair up into a makeshift ponytail, holding it with a strong hand while she sucked him. It was so hot, it made me sweat. He controlled her pace, and the leather seats protested when he thrust up into her mouth.

All the air in the interior of the limo seemed to have disappeared, and in this vacuum, electricity crackled with intensity as both Logan and I approached orgasm. I wasn't trying to time it with him, but I also wasn't in control. Dominic was, absolutely.

"Who's going to come first?" His gravel whisper asked. "I think it should be you."

Desire burned across my skin, glossing it, and I hungered for my release. Everything ached and focused in on the end goal. The tingling, lightweight sensation that happened just before orgasm fluttered in my belly.

"Mmm..." I moaned through Dominic's hand, and let the pleasure take me. I convulsed in his embrace, slowed my own touch, and pressed my fingers hard to my pulsing clit. My eyes pinched shut and everything felt warm and amazing as I exploded.

As it faded, I inhaled a breath slowly through my nose, and the hand fell away from my mouth.

"Yes, just like that," Logan said through clenched teeth. "I'm gonna come." His grip guided her to go faster, and faster, and... "Shit, shit!"

His moans built into a crescendo and peaked, and he held her firm as he came, her jaw locked around him. It prolonged the aftershocks of my orgasm, even as Dominic's fingers retreated. But when he withdrew, it took the last of the energy from my body. Exhaustion stormed in and made itself home.

What about Dominic?

I set a hand on the bulge of his pants, stroking down, but he took my hand in his and stopped me.

"Can I be honest?" he said. "I'm fucking tired. I need a raincheck, devil woman."

He couldn't be more perfect if he'd tried. "Thank God. I am, too. You just saved yourself from a lackluster blow job."

His eyebrow lifted. "Blow job's still a blow job." But his arms tightened around my waist, holding me close. "Tomorrow. You better give me your A-game."

I shrugged and tossed my hair over a shoulder. "I don't know. I don't just give that to anybody."

The embrace was gone, only so he could flick my tattoo and deliver the tiny sting that reminded me how much I loved him. Even though he knew I didn't need it.

Chapter SEVEN

I stared at my phone, gnashed my teeth, and slowly lifted my gaze to meet Dominic's. "They're late."

"Give them a minute. You know how traffic can be."

We sat in the back of the crowded restaurant and nursed drinks while we waited for my parents to arrive. I'd made the call yesterday morning while Dominic hovered over me, ensuring that a decent effort was put in on my part. And I couldn't fault him for wanting this, but I hated it. My parents were going to disappoint us, and although I wasn't responsible, I still felt that way by association.

The waiter came by and asked if we wanted to order lunch, but Dominic shook his head and the waiter left.

"You think it'd be rude to order without them?" I asked. Dominic's expression was pointed, but I shrugged. "Well, I think it's fucking rude that they can't tell us they're running behind."

I was halfway through my second glass of wine when my phone rang. I glanced at the number and groaned. "One guess who it is." I swiped to answer the call and tried not to seethe. "Hey, where are you?"

"Payton," my mother said. "Your father's in a deposition that's taking a lot longer than he thought it would. Are you already at the restaurant?"

Was I—? *Seriously?* "Yeah. You said one o'clock."

She sighed. "I don't know when he's going to be finished, and he's got to be in court by three. This case has been such a mess, I told him he should have given it to one of the other partners."

"So you're not coming."

From across the table, Dominic's blue eyes studied me, gauging my response. All he wanted was to meet my parents. We'd flown ten thousand miles from Japan, and they couldn't make it twenty blocks from my father's law firm.

"We were looking forward to it," my mom said, "but it's been such a busy week. I'm sorry. I feel just awful about it."

"Yeah?" I was done with this bullshit. "You should feel awful." I pressed the *End Call* button and dropped my phone on the table. Surely my mother was on the other end wondering what had happened. I'd never talked to her like that before, but I'd also never felt more let down by them.

"I'm sorry," Dominic said.

His unnecessary apology only made me angrier. "*You're* sorry? For what? Wanting my parents not to be dicks?"

I said it too loud and the couple at the table next to us glanced over.

"No more wine for you." Dominic gave me a lopsided smile. "You know, it's easier to talk like that when no one around us speaks English."

"I told you this would happen."

He blinked, but his face remained unchanged. "You

did." He flipped open his menu casually. "So, we tried, Payton. We'll see if they change their attitude when they want to see their grandkids."

Grandkids.

We both wanted children, and we'd talked about it in the future, but it continued to throw me off balance how settled and comfortable he was with the idea. Sometimes I'd catch myself staring with disbelief at the enormous ring on my finger. I was engaged, I had to remind myself. I'd found another person who willingly wanted to be a part of my life. Shocking.

His carefree demeanor, and the lunch we eventually ordered, diffused some of my anger. It was pointless to get worked up, and I tried to emulate Dominic's easy mood.

"So, I've been thinking," I said as we finished up our plates. "We both technically won the bet about Evie and Logan."

Dominic leaned back in his chair and crossed his arms. "How do you figure that?"

"The no-sex rule. It didn't get broken."

A lazy smile grew on his lips. "Fine, devil woman. I'll have lunch with Joseph, but only because you want us to. Let's be clear. You did not win that bet."

"Whatever." I climbed out of my chair, and was about to tell him I was heading for the restroom, when something caught my eye. Not something, but *someone*.

Holy shit.

He wove through the tables, moving quickly toward me, a blur in an expensive suit. "Payton."

"What the fuck?" I stared in disbelief.

He grinned, surprised. "Wow, nice language." His glance went from top to bottom. "And, wow. You look great."

Dominic's hand was warm on my waist, but his expression painted in a scowl at this man he didn't know. I would have laughed if I could get over what I was seeing.

"You must be the fiancé. I'm Kyle McCreary." My brother extended a hand.

Once the information settled in, the tension in Dominic's shoulders relaxed and a smile broke on his face. He took Kyle's hand and shook it. "Hey, yeah. Dominic Ward."

"Okay," I said. "What are you doing here?"

"Mom told me what happened. I thought I'd see if I could catch you before you left."

There was a thin gloss of sweat on Kyle's forehead as if he'd hurried, and the purple plaid tie he wore with his gray suit was askew.

"So you ran from New York all the way to this restaurant?"

Kyle's soft smile froze. "No, I live here now." He pushed his suitcoat back so he could rest his hands on his hips and catch his breath. "You didn't know?"

He looked so different from the last time I'd seen him, which had been . . . when? My college graduation? Kyle's hair was more like Dad's, the color of maple syrup. He'd let it go long on the top and it was a little wild. Soft curls turned up at the ends. I couldn't tell if he'd skipped shaving for the last three days, or if it was perfectly maintained scruff.

Either way, it was a good look on him.

My arms moved without thought, and suddenly I was hugging him. Kyle stood straight and immobile, confused. My family did *not* hug. But then again, I'd always been the black sheep.

"No, Mom didn't tell me," I said. "She's *too busy*, I guess." I stepped back from him and curled into Dominic's embrace. "When did you move?"

"About six weeks ago. Dad got me a position with his firm."

"What happened to New York?"

Kyle's eyes clouded with an emotion I couldn't interpret. He looked . . . unhappy? But in a flash, the emotion was replaced with an empty one. "That's a story for later." His gaze held mine. "Look, I can't stay. My schedule's crazy while they're bringing me up to speed on my caseload, but . . . hell. We haven't seen each other in a while."

We certainly hadn't. My older brother and I weren't close growing up. I'd done my own thing while Kyle had been the golden boy. I didn't envy him; the crown seemed heavy. Mom and Dad laid enormous pressure on him, so I understood when he'd high-tailed it out of Chicago, not a week after graduating law school. My parents felt disrespected he hadn't come to the firm that carried the McCreary name.

But that had been years ago. Now he was back?

"So you ran twenty blocks in a suit to see me?" I asked.

"Mom said you were upset." He took a deep breath and smoothed a hand down his tie. "Mom and Dad don't get it. They think their stuff is more important than anyone else's. I used to try really hard to make them understand, and honestly, my life got so much easier once I stopped."

My mouth dropped open. It was the most honest I'd ever heard him, and he made his living spinning truths and twisting words.

"I also came to meet Dominic." Kyle's focus shifted to my fiancé. "As her brother, I'm supposed to threaten you with bodily harm if you don't treat her right, but that's not really my style. So enjoy my threat of litigation instead. I'm very good, and it wouldn't be pleasant."

"Aw, you're sweet," I said, my voice mocking. "But Dominic's smart. He knows if he fucks up with me, I'd be his biggest threat."

"Yes," Dominic said instantly.

Kyle blinked again at the profanity. Not like he was offended, but more amused. Shit, how far apart had we'd been these last few years? He barely knew me anymore, and I'd never really known him.

"Okay, well, that's good, I guess." Kyle fiddled with his watch and checked the time. "I have to run. As in, literally."

"Thank you for coming," I said, hoping my voice matched how sincere I felt, because I was a little blown away.

"Should we grab drinks some night this week?" Dominic asked, but Kyle shook his head.

"I'd like that, but everything's a mess with the move. You two will be back for good in a few months though, right? We could do it then."

"Sure."

We said our goodbyes, and I watched Kyle go. It was such a simple gesture for him to come over, and yet it meant so much.

Dominic had a strange half-smile on his face.

"What is it?" I asked.

"Running here and back just to say hello. Your parents don't get it, but your brother does."

"Yeah," I said. *Who would have thought?*

The premium leather of my driver's seat was buttery soft. I'd narrowly avoided reunion tears when I'd picked my car up from Logan's place. Well, *technically,* our place. Evie and Logan would move out in mid-December so Dominic and I could move in when we returned from Japan.

I felt bad about kicking them out, but only for thirty seconds. The view was to die for, and Logan had known this day was coming since leasing the place from his friend.

"It looks different in the daylight," Dominic said, gesturing to the blindfold club entrance. He wasn't wrong. The black door looked smaller, and the wear on the façade seemed greater in the harsh light.

"Yeah, this place is way less sexy during the day." A fact I'd discovered the first time Joseph had asked me to fill in for him. I hadn't a clue why Joseph wanted to meet here now, but since the club was a good twenty-minute drive from our hotel, and I had my hands on my Jaguar F-Type, it was fine with me.

"Any chance you'd let me drive the car back to the hotel when we leave?" Dominic's hopeful expression wasn't enough to pry my grip from the steering wheel.

He hadn't driven a car in almost two years. "No way, get your own."

"Half of this car will be mine when we're married."

I shut off the engine and let my expression go serious. "Yeah, the passenger half."

We hurried across the street and through the front door that Joseph left unlocked for us. It was dark except for the security as we strolled through the bar and down the hallway of doors. The silence and poor lighting further detracted from the sex appeal.

To the left were the holding lounges, and to the right were the client rooms. I'd met Dominic in Room One. A smile warmed on my lips as we passed the door decorated with the brass six, the room where Dominic asked me to be his wife.

"Joseph?" I called, leading Dominic upstairs.

"In here."

Not in his office, but across the hall in the large dressing room. He stood by the bar lining the far wall, his back turned to us. His suit jacket was cast aside on a chair, and as he poured himself a glass of whiskey, I could see his sleeves had been rolled back. This was as close to casual as Joseph got.

"Hey."

My voice forced him to turn. He probably appeared composed and maintained to Dominic, but like the last time I'd seen Joseph, there were faint edges around his eyes. He looked . . . weary. Not that I'd say that to him. Joseph was all about power, and he'd view it as weakness.

He smiled. "You got him to agree to come."

"Of course," I said. "My boy-toy does whatever I tell him to."

The snap on my hip was sharp and biting. Dull pain lingered on my tattoo, so I glared up at the blue eyes watching me. "Okay, ow."

Dominic looked smug. "Watch it."

"You watch it," I echoed back like a four-year-old.

Joseph carried his drink in one hand and strode toward us, pretending he hadn't just witnessed the immature exchange. "Dominic," he said. "I'm Joseph Monsato."

"I remember." My fiancé's words were tight. "Everything about that night was pretty hard to forget. You know, except for those ten minutes after the bouncer's right hook."

They'd met face to face in the front lounge when Dominic first arrived at the club almost a year ago. It was protocol with walk-ins, plus Joseph liked to evaluate potential clients to match them with the right girl. That meeting had been fine, according to Dominic, but the way he'd left the club was still a sore subject. He'd spent the whole night trying to find me, his head throbbing with a black eye, all because of Joseph.

"I'm sorry about what happened," Joseph said, his expression genuine. "I didn't handle it well when Payton said she wanted to leave. Your fiancée was a big part of this place, and also my friend, and . . . I wasn't sure how the fuck I was going to get on without her."

Joseph didn't mean it sexually, of that I was sure. Yet his admission made my breath stall in my lungs. When I'd left the club, I hadn't just quit, I'd effectively abandoned Joseph. I was at a loss for words, which had to be a fucking first.

"It was good, though," Joseph continued. "For me, and most definitely for her."

Dominic shifted his stance. He didn't seem to be faring much better than I was with the seesaw emotions between resentment and surprise. "Uh, yeah."

Joseph's attention sought mine. "I bet you want to know why I asked you here."

"The question had crossed my mind."

"I need a favor, and unfortunately, I need it from both of you."

Well, he was just full of surprises today. "What is it?"

The amber liquid sloshed in Joseph's drink as he swirled his glass. "I hired a new girl, and I can't get a read on her." He paused to take a sip. "Usually I can tell whether or not they'd be good, but this one . . ."

"How'd she do with her—" I wasn't about to remind Dominic how the girls at the club got their spots. Several months ago I'd had too much vodka, or 'truth serum' as he called it, and spilled all the gritty details about the club. "With her audition?"

"Christ," Dominic growled.

But Joseph's face was stoic. "She didn't audition.

Regan's only interested in being a sales assistant. She's made it clear she won't get on the table."

As far as I knew, that was a first. All girls started on the table. "Why not?"

"She says she has a boyfriend, but I don't think that's her reason."

"Okay, what is?"

"She's not submissive," Joseph said.

I could sense Dominic's impatience with all of this, and tried to get right to it. "So, what's the favor?"

"I'm hoping you'll get on the table," he said, his dark gaze trapping mine. "And let Regan negotiate the deal when Dominic tries to buy you."

Chapter
EIGHT

Regan was a redhead, her hair fire engine red with streaks of copper. She had gorgeous, big blue eyes and high cheekbones, and a slender frame. But beneath her simple black suit dress, I could see power lurked. This woman had a strict workout regimen.

Her sleek nose and bow lips made her look regal. She was beautiful, which was good. Her looks would help her during negotiations. A little older than me, but still young.

"You've done this before?" I asked her as I stripped off my clothes and hung them in the empty, open-faced locker in the dressing room. Dominic had been sequestered into one of the holding rooms downstairs, while Joseph went to his office.

My fiancé hadn't been thrilled with this plan, but I felt like I owed Joseph. I'd abandoned him twice in the last year, first when I'd quit, and once again when I'd gone back to Japan. So I told Dominic I wanted this, and gave him the reminder that he'd be running the show when I was on the table. Total control over me.

So, he was on board.

Regan's voice was pleasant. "I shadowed with Nina and Tara several times. I know I'm new, but trust me. I'll get the most I can out of him."

Even though it came off sounding arrogant, I liked

it. Sales were all about confidence, and this woman had it in spades.

I slipped an arm into the silk robe while her gaze lingered at the tattoo on my hip, but she said nothing. She seemed comfortable when I'd gotten naked, not staring, but not averting her eyes either. Like she was assessing me as a product, which was good. I dug through my black hole of a purse until I located a tube of lipstick and went to the mirror to apply it.

"You're sure you're up for this?" she asked. "Joseph said you haven't been back very long."

I pressed my lips together, spreading the color evenly. We'd decided for a cover story that I'd left Dominic back in Japan, returned to Chicago bitter from the breakup, and flat broke. I was ready to get back to the blindfold club and start earning money.

"Fuck yeah. I might be a little rusty, but I haven't forgotten what to do." I gave her a wink. Not that there was all that much to it. I'd be bound, blindfolded, and not supposed to speak.

"All right. Let's go make some money." She hooked in her earpiece and motioned toward the door.

If Regan was nervous about her first solo sale, she didn't show it. Her heels clicked steadily over the floor when she pushed open the door to Room Two and led me inside. She moved with practiced efficiency to prepare. First, the lights, then the thermostat, and finally she went to the cushioned table in the center.

A drawer squeaked as I slipped the robe off and hung

it on the hook. Regan already had the straps tethered to the anchors on the table when I made my way toward her.

"Joseph mentioned the client is already in the holding room," she said, subtly telling me not to dawdle. Wealthy men didn't wait for pussy. "Did he tell you anything about the appointment? I figure he's someone important for Joseph to schedule in the middle of the week."

"Maybe," I said with forced casualness. It was hilarious how excited I was about the favor. Dominic and I were both going to enjoy this role-play.

Regan rushed through the final stages of setup so I was bound and had the blindfold in place, and she signaled Joseph through her comm that we were ready. There was no sound from her other than her soft breathing. She didn't bother to move to the chair in the corner to wait, knowing it wouldn't be long.

In the dark and quiet, my body began to respond. Goosebumps pebbled on my skin and anticipation hardened my nipples into knots. I licked my lips, waiting impatiently for him.

"Good afternoon, sir," Regan's voice purred.

I hadn't heard the door open, but it shut behind him and Dominic shuffled a few steps closer. My legs slid together, rubbing my knees against each other as desire corded around me. Would he leave the blindfold on this time? The straps, I was sure. I'd called the shots both times we'd been here before, and he wasn't going to give me an opportunity to do it a third time.

"Do you like what you see?" Regan asked sincerely.

Not pushing, not yet.

"Yeah, she's pretty cute."

My face scrunched under the blindfold. What the fuck was that, *cute*? I held my tongue, but I'd let him hear about it later. He was probably grinning at how hilarious he thought he was. That was, if he wasn't blushing.

"Pretty cute?" Regan's words were dubious. "I think she's gorgeous."

"Yeah, all right, she's really fucking hot." *Better, Dominic.*

"You two would make quite the pair. It looks like you're in fantastic shape, if you don't mind me saying. Do you work out, play sports?"

Good. Regan used the code to communicate that he was attractive when she dropped the sports mention.

"No sports. I'm more into lifting. So, how does this work?"

She paused. "You haven't been to the club before?"

"No." Dominic took a step closer. "I almost didn't come in. This place didn't look like I expected it to."

It wasn't all that much of a lie, and I appreciated the detail. He was doing a decent job of selling it.

"Well, I'm glad you did. Is that beautiful Jaguar out front yours?"

"Sure is."

I could hear the fucking smile in his voice, and it was insanely difficult not to jolt against the restraints or call him out. Oh, he was going to *get it* when these straps were off.

"Nice," she said. "Fifty thousand."

He gave a sharp noise of surprise. "Are you asking if my car was fifty thousand dollars, or is that the price—"

"It's for her."

Holy shit, what the fuck was Regan doing?

"That's . . . too much." He stumbled over the words, as if he wasn't sure what was going on. Yeah, me too.

"You're saying you don't think she's worth that?"

A frustrated sigh slipped out. He'd told me long ago the negotiations made him queasy. He didn't like assigning a dollar value to me. This was supposed to be fun. *Pretend.* Her question made it a little too real.

"I'm saying . . . I'd feel more comfortable paying five."

Her heels clicked as she glided closer to him. "I understand." Her warm hand rested lightly on my ankle. The indication that she thought he was willing to pay a lot more, which he had agreed to once.

Her hand squeezed, prompting me to respond. I shook my head.

"I'm sorry, she's not willing to accept the offer. Would you like to try again? How about sixty thousand?"

"What? That's more."

I couldn't understand what her game was, and broke the rule about staying quiet. I tried not to hiss it at her. "What are you doing?"

"Joseph told me to try to get as much out of the client as I could." Her direct voice was stunning. "I believe this man would pay every last cent he had for you." *Oh my God.* "Am I wrong?"

The question seemed to be for Dominic. He

sighed. "Nope."

"You're her boyfriend?" she asked.

"Fiancé."

"Fuck," I said, squirming against the straps. "What tipped you off?"

"Lots of things. He didn't look at your tattoo, which is interesting, so that made me think he'd already seen it. There's no security on the premises, which says Joseph trusts this man with you." She paused. "Also, I could tell he lied about the car. Even if I couldn't, it was too much coincidence. I saw the Jaguar logo on your keyring as you were going through your purse upstairs."

A feminine hand was on my wrists, tugging at the Velcro.

"The biggest giveaway," she continued, "is the way he looks at you. Can't take his eyes off of you."

The command from Dominic was quiet, but firm. "Stop. I'll do that."

Yeah, he'd undo my restraints . . . when he was good and ready. I took in a deep breath. "Tell Joseph he should hire you."

She gave a half-laugh. "He just did." She must have meant through the comm in her ear. "Have fun, you two."

Heels tapped out on the hard floor, growing quieter with each step, and the door fell shut. I flinched when fingers skimmed across my belly and up between the valley of my breasts. He gripped my chin and set his soft lips against mine.

"I would, you know," Dominic said. "Pay every last

cent I have for you, Payton."

"I told you, I don't want your money."

His hot mouth sucked and licked at the base of my throat as it journeyed downward. "Yeah? What do you want?"

"For starters, I want my ring back. And then I want your cock."

He chuckled and the mouth vanished. The cold ring was slipped back onto its home on my finger, and I clenched my hand tight around it. It'd been off for twenty minutes, but it felt like eons.

"Okay, now that cock."

His lips were back at my collarbone, inching over my skin. "You," the stubble of his unshaven face rubbed against my breasts, "are not . . . *fucking* in charge."

"Shit!" I cried as he nipped at the underside of my breast, hard enough it might have left a crescent shaped mark. His physical mark on me to match the emotional one he'd left. Dominic stained my soul, and I loved it. Electricity spider-webbed from the sting, and my veins flooded with heat.

My hands curled around ribbons holding me down as his fingernails scored painlessly across my stomach in a straight line toward my pussy. His light touch was worse than his firm one. The ache choked my lungs and left my head swirling with need.

Inch by inch.

His mouth followed his fingers down and he inhaled deeply, like he was trying to memorize my scent. The pads of his fingers worked over the inside of my thighs, my hips, and dragged slowly from one spot to another just above my slit. Teasing. Tormenting.

"Touch me," I whispered.

He didn't. His palms smoothed down my legs and back up again. I urged my knees apart and the leather protested quietly. The throb in my clit was intense, fueled by his warm breath that I could feel pouring over me.

"Dominic," I whined.

Those fucking hands continued to explore and linger, never straying to where I was desperate for them. His lips skimmed the inside of my knee. Sparks danced across my nerves as two fingers brushed upward in a line along my thigh, starting a tremble in my legs.

"Please." I begged it on a shuddering breath.

"This is how I like you. Watching you trying to keep it together." There was another nip on my thigh, but this one was soft and seductive. "Let's play a little game, Payton. I'm going to undo one of your straps."

It was hard to think through the fog of lust. He was going to set me free? The use of one hand meant I could easily undo the other strap or pull off the blindfold. I'd only have the illusion of restraint.

"I'm going to make you come," he said. He kissed the spot where my leg joined my body. The muscles low in my stomach clenched in response, so hard it was almost painful. "If you touch me, or yourself, you don't get to come the rest of the day."

I swallowed a gulp of air and bit down on my bottom

lip. I almost preferred that he keep me bound. I didn't trust myself. But the Velcro tugged open with a loud scratchy noise, and his hand closed on my wrist, pinning it to the mattress-top.

"It's simple. Your hand stays here. Can you obey?"

My chest was heaving and my heart raced. "Yes, Sir."

He issued a noise of approval. I didn't call him Sir often as if he were my Dom and mean it. I liked rationing the word so it carried more power and weight when used.

"*Yes*," I cried. My back arched up off the table and my head tipped back. His soft, sinful tongue licked and swirled. It fluttered on my clit. I probably looked like a woman possessed when he fucked me with his mouth, but it was true. I was completely possessed by him. Two thick fingers crept inside. The first inch. And another. Behind closed eyelids, colors spun with my pleasure.

But the warmth of his mouth retreated, causing me to collapse back against the cushion-top.

"Oh . . . my . . . *fuck*."

He wasn't playing fair. A third finger nudged down, touching my asshole while his fingers were fucking my pussy. I swallowed hard, and commanded my hand to stay in place. I wanted to rub my clit as his finger began to intrude there, filling me full. My orgasms with anal were much more intense, but I wouldn't get there on penetration alone.

I began to writhe when he had two fingers in each entrance. His languid pace was diabolical, and I pictured him bent over the table between my legs, propped up on one arm as he fucked me with the other. His gorgeous eyes would be watching my every move. Every gasp of breath I took.

My head turned and I moaned it into the side of my arm. "Oh, God, please."

It was killing me not to set my fingers on my swollen clit. It would probably take me two circles of my frantic fingers and I'd come apart. He knew this. He was pushing me as he liked to do.

"You're so fucking hot, I can't stand it," he said in his rough, deep voice.

I cried out in relief as his other hand cupped my pussy, his thumb rolling circles on the nub that was the center of my pleasure.

"Scream for me," he commanded.

Holy shit, I did. It ripped from my throat and echoed in the soundproof room, so only he could hear how much ecstasy he'd drawn out of my body. I convulsed on his fingers as bliss tore me apart, and the sensation went on.

And on.

Oh my God.

I screamed again as the second wave of pleasure crashed into me, leaving my mind blank. All I could do was shudder and endure as my body took control. Flashes of white decorated my eyelids.

"Fuck," he groaned. "Your pussy's gonna break my fingers."

There was no response I could give. No biting remark. I had to focus on pulling air in through clenched teeth. He'd gotten me breathing so hard I'd come close to passing out. The hand slid away. His zipper rang out. The table shook as he climbed on it.

His voice was pure sex. "Here's the cock you asked for."

He didn't give me any rest. His fat dick impaled me in a single thrust. My mouth fell open, but no sound came out and my heart refused to work properly. It slammed in my chest just as fast as he slammed into me, and it burned so good.

His clothed body pressed to my naked one, and my nipples rubbed against the cotton of his t-shirt. I loved feeling his weight on me. Then he shifted, taking it away for a moment, and when his body pressed back down, it was warm skin on mine. He'd pushed his shirt up so we could have delicious contact.

The fingers of my unbound wrist flexed and curled back into a fist. I yearned to touch him, or to push my blindfold up so I could watch as he fucked me. Whimpers flowed from my mouth. Desperate, pathetic noises that only seemed to make his cock harder and his thrusts deeper.

"You feel so fucking good," I mumbled into the side of his neck. The flutters in my belly began once more, and I was quaking beneath him.

"You ready to come again?" His voice was corrupt.

My head bobbed up and down, nodding violently.

One hand slipped beneath me, grabbing a handful of my ass and squeezing just to the edge of pain. He slammed his hips against me, driving his cock at a furious pace. "Then fucking do it."

I moaned as he shoved me over the edge into euphoria. Another of my screams filled the room, but this one was followed by his loud groan, and it set off a series of jerks from him. His cock pulsed inside me, one wave after another of heated bliss.

The tense muscles pressed against mine began to relax as he recovered from his orgasm. "Shit, our American sex is epic."

A short laugh fell out of me. "Our Japanese sex isn't a joke either."

"We should teach classes." He faked seriousness. "People could learn a lot from us."

"Right. Like how not to lie about your fiancée's car being yours." A finger tugged the blindfold off and I blinked at my vision suddenly being restored.

"It'll be mine eventually." His voice was heavy with meaning and his eyes glinted.

He was right in every sense. He pushed me, always getting his way in the end, and I *loved* every minute of it.

I loved it almost as much as I loved him.

Chapter NINE

EVIE

Processional music broadcasted softly from the small speaker in the cramped bridal room. It sounded tinny through the electronics, but I hoped it was beautiful for the guests sitting in the pews in the nave of the church. I was sure it was. Logan had picked the quartet himself.

Holy crap, it was really happening.

Logan's mom probably had the same thought. She'd been waiting for this day a long time. For years, everyone had assumed it'd be a lithe blonde marching down the aisle, not a brunette with thick thighs.

Why the hell was I thinking about his ex? I was a jittery mess, all nervous and excited and happy. I couldn't wait to see him, and I couldn't fucking wait to become his wife.

My gaze was glued to Payton, who held her bouquet of blue hydrangeas and white roses in one hand, and fiddled with the top of her bridesmaid dress. I'd let the girls pick their own, the only stipulation being that the dress was solid black. She'd chosen a strapless one that had a deep V notched in the center of the neckline, revealing her ample cleavage. By her standards, the dress was tame, but the priest was going to have a heart attack.

"Don't forget," I said to her. "Flowers up here." I held

my bouquet up high over my chest. I need to crack a joke to distract from my nerves.

She smirked. "Are you insane? I'm not covering my best feature."

My father cleared his throat and Payton sobered, falling into line with the rest of my bridesmaids while we moved to the narthex. Only a set of double doors stood between Logan and me now. At the front of the line, Jamie disappeared through them with her arm linked to Logan's half-brother Garrett.

Payton had corrected Jamie at the rehearsal dinner last night when my coworker friend called me Evie. God, my best friend's little jealous streak was so funny. It's not like I'd demoted Payton's best friend status, but Jamie and I had become friends over the past year. Plus she had been awesome at helping plan the wedding on a budget. Thank God the Stones offered to pay for half of it. I was so blessed, and my family was grateful.

"Oh, no," I whispered to my father. "Don't you dare. If you start, I start, and I won't be able to stop." Tears stung and threatened to spill.

He wiped at his eyes and pinched the bridge of his nose. "I'm fine. I've got it together. It's just thirty feet." Since his tone was unsure, I stared up at the ceiling, desperate to drain the tears back.

Nick, Logan's brother, was the best man, but it made more sense for him to walk down the aisle with his wife Hilary, who was also a bridesmaid. Plus, this left Payton and Dominic to walk together. My heartbeat ratcheted up another level as Hilary and Nick disappeared into the church.

My knees were soft and uncooperative as Dominic stepped into view, offering his arm to my maid of honor. "You look beautiful," he said as she threaded her hand through the crook of his elbow. "Oh, and you, Payton, you look nice, too."

She turned, flashed a grin back at me, and stepped off with Dominic.

"Thirty feet," my dad mumbled to himself, like he was trying to get pumped up.

My heart launched into my throat, blocking air as the song ended and the first strings of the wedding march began. I wasn't sure who was leaning on whom for support; both of us were shaking.

The doors swung open with the swell in the music, revealing the standing rows of friends and family who'd come to celebrate Logan's and my union. Every pair of eyes was on me, except for my father's. He was probably counting the steps as we moved forward.

No amount of visualization could have prepared me emotionally for this moment.

I'd seen Logan in a tuxedo before, and it had made me weak in the ovaries, but now he incinerated them. They didn't stand a chance against his perfect three-piece black suit, a formal black bow tied at his neck.

His focus was one hundred percent on me. There could be fireworks going off all around, we wouldn't have noticed. They couldn't compete with the fireworks between us anyway.

Logan's lips parted and shoulders lifted in a deep breath. Had I ever seen him this stunned before? My perfectly controlled man seemed to be struggling. The thoughts he held were loud on his face. He wanted to storm up the aisle and whirl me into his arms. He'd like to kiss me hard, and probably fuck me harder.

Oh, God. I'd just thought about fucking while at church. I was going to hell.

The enormous skirt of my A-line dress swished as we ambled across the white aisle runner at a measured pace. My dad was rushing and I tensed my arm, trying to get him to slow down. There was so much to take in, I didn't want to miss any of it. Every step brought me closer to the man I loved, and I wanted to celebrate them each as a victory.

As the distance between us shortened, the depth in Logan's dark eyes grew. His expression filled with so much love, it was overwhelming. My bottom lip and chin trembled as I teetered right on the edge.

No, no, no... I did not want to cry. Why did people cry when they were happy? I fought to pull the corners of my mouth back into a smile.

"Ten, nine..."

Oh, good God, my father was literally counting under his breath. His stage fright was a welcomed distraction, and it was like a countdown to the moment I'd be with my groom.

"Five... four..." Logan straightened and his broad shoulders pulled back as he inched forward, as if he couldn't wait and wanted to meet me halfway.

"Three . . . two . . . one."

Logan's hand was extended to my father and the men shook. I leaned in, tilting my head as my dad kissed my cheek.

"I love you, Evelyn. Your mother and I are so happy for you." I closed my eyes, squeezing back fresh tears. "And I'm outta here."

My eyes popped open, and I choked on my laugh as my dad scurried behind me, trying not to trip over my cathedral veil. My gaze turned back and found Logan's. His hand clasped mine and our fingers laced together. We turned toward the altar and went forward, together.

It was a blur after that. Readings, vows, and the rings. I slipped the silver band on Logan's left hand, and . . . yup, definitely going to hell. More impure thoughts at church. The band symbolizing his commitment to me was undeniably sexy. Our gazes and hands locked together.

The priest's baritone voice echoed in the vaulted ceilings. "You may now share your first kiss as husband and wife."

Even though I knew it was coming, the moment still caught me off guard. I wanted to lick my lips, which felt sticky from the long-lasting lipstick the makeup artist had applied this morning, yet Logan didn't give me time. As soon as he had the go-ahead, his fingertips glided over my cheek, gently drawing me in. His mouth lowered to mine and stole my breath. Soft, warm lips moved unhurried, taking as much time as he wanted, teasing me with a hint of tongue. I melted against his kiss as I always did. It was as shockingly good as it had been our first time that wild, out of control night outside the blindfold club.

No, wait, this was better. A million times better because he was my husband.

His kiss left me woozy, and I swayed when his hands retreated, my body mourning their absence. It was momentary, because he wrapped his hand around mine, holding me steady. His dark, intense eyes sparkled, helping further to pin me back in place.

The ceremony drew to a close, and it was impossible to catch our breath. Pictures. The receiving line. The stretch limo that carried us with our bridal party to the Opulent Hotel where our reception would be.

We'd squeezed together to all fit in the limo, and with my enormous dress, I was practically sitting on Logan's lap.

"You look amazing, wife." He murmured it against the side of my neck, and I giggled.

"You look pretty amazing yourself, husband."

Being in the limo with him was a dangerous reminder of our evening last Saturday, and I shuddered with anticipation. Dinner, dancing, and then we'd be upstairs in the honeymoon suite, completely alone. No more closet or bathroom doors shielding his gorgeous body from my eyes, and no more self-imposed rules of keeping it in our pants.

By the time we arrived at the hotel, cocktail hour was nearly over. Payton hurried to bustle my dress in the handicapped stall of the bathroom while I slammed a bottle of water.

"There you are," Logan said when we emerged, as if we'd been in there for a century. "We need to line up for introductions." He threw a pointed look at Payton. "You're letting her fall behind schedule, McCreary."

She snatched a glass of white wine off a server's tray. "Yeah? I dare you to figure out the ribbons of her bustle faster than I did."

"The only thing I'm going to concern myself with Evie's dress," Logan said, "is how fast I can get her out of it."

I laughed, but it froze in my throat as my grandmother's head turned our direction. *Shit!* A light smile breezed on her lips, and she ... *oh my God*. She winked.

Logan and I scarfed down our dinners so we could spend as much time as possible mingling among the tables of our guests. I'd been to weddings where the bride and groom never once spoke to me and was determined not to have that happen at mine.

"I don't want to whine," I whispered to Logan as we began our first dance together. We were all alone on the dancefloor while our friends and family watched. "But my feet kind of hurt."

"Yeah? Mine too."

I had one hand on his chest and the other resting on the back of his neck as we swayed to the love song that filled the ballroom. Logan took my hand, held it away and led me through a turn under his arm. As I came back into his embrace, I stared up at him, wide-eyed. "What's this? It's not eight-grade dancing."

"My mom informed me I had to up my game. That's

at least a tenth grade move I just gave you."

"Nice."

I was torn between not wanting the evening to end and my desire for it to be over so we could go upstairs. We laughed with our family, posed for pictures with friends, and ate a piece of our wedding cake.

My feet were aching and screaming for relief as the deejay played the final song of the night. Our crowd had thinned once the bar closed at eleven, and as soon as the song was over, the lights in the ballroom brightened. It had been an amazing day, but also exhausting.

Dominic's arms were tight around Payton's waist. "Logan," he said, his tone serious, "it's been a while for you. Let me know if you need any pointers for the wedding night."

"Thanks, Dominic. By the way, go fuck yourself."

Payton laughed. "He has me for that."

As soon as the elevator doors sealed us in alone together, Logan was on me. One warm hand splayed on the bare skin of my back while his other gripped my ass tightly, pressing me into him, crushing my dress. He held me into his kiss that was an assault on all fronts. My heart, mind, and body *needed* this man. My hand dove inside his tuxedo jacket, seeking the hardened muscles beneath the crisp dress shirt and three-button black vest.

"You have too many clothes on, boss."

"I'm fucking aware."

We hit our floor, he grabbed my hand, and tugged me down the hallway.

"Slow down," I gasped. "Not all of us are runners." He was dragging me along at break-neck speed.

"Is it faster if I carry you?"

I had no idea if he was kidding or not. We'd been together more than a year, and it wasn't any easier to tell. "I dunno, maybe."

A yelp escaped when his hands gripped my waist, lifting me, and not the sexy swept-up-into-his-arms kind, but the thrown-over-the-shoulder, caveman style kind of carry.

"Shit," he groaned. "Your skirt is huge." He banded an arm around my thighs, tucking the fabric out of his way so he could see, and took off. I bounced on his shoulder and the shorter, elbow-length veil I'd switched into for the reception hung down, trailing on the carpet.

"You don't like my dress?"

"I didn't say that. You took my breath away, Evie."

My heart thumped in my chest and my face warmed with a flush, but that also could have been the blood rushing to my head because I was upside-down.

"Hey, put me down before you hurt yourself." Although, if I were honest, I kind of liked this. His 'I have to have you now' attitude was seriously hot.

We were through the door and into the honeymoon suite. I couldn't see much, but the room was softly glowing with flickering light. His strong arms braced me as I slowly slid down his body until my feet were back on the ground. The veil was flipped over my head, and Logan lifted it, brushing it back.

"Are you thirsty? There's champagne."

"Oh?" I turned in his arms to face the room, "....my God."

A white, king-sized bed was against the left wall, decorated with a gold satin comforter and eggplant purple accent pillows. Mirrored, square lamps were perched on the nightstands. Everything was elegant and luxurious.

The back wall was like our apartment. Floor to ceiling glass with a view to die for, only this wasn't North Beach, it was the heart of the city, and the yellow-orange windows glowed in the night.

Also glowing were glass votive candles that lined just about every flat surface in the room. No lights were on, and it was breathtaking. I stood motionless as Logan went to the ice bucket and pulled out the bottle of champagne.

My desire for him was so strong I could taste it, but instead I remained still, watching him open the bottle and pour me a glass. I gestured to the room. "Did you arrange this?"

The only answer he gave me was a half-smile, but it confirmed he had. He held out the glass of champagne and I took it, letting my gaze fall to the other focal point in the room . . . the large Jacuzzi tub. It sat opposite the bed in a corner, the walls wrapped in mirror and the tile ledge around it was covered with more flickering candles.

It was romantic and seductive.

My gaze went back to him, starting at his feet and drifting upward over that sexy tuxedo, all the way until I could meet his eyes. Those chocolate brown eyes had been my undoing our first night together, and they were just as devastating now. Especially since they seemed to be filled with the same sordid thoughts he'd had then.

He poured another glass for himself but didn't take a sip. His intense focus was on me. "Lose the dress."

Chapter TEN

I swallowed thickly and smiled. I was eager, but . . . "I'm going to need your help."

Logan took a sip of his champagne and set it down, then shrugged out of his jacket. He tossed it on the chair nearby, and I'd learned he only disregarded his neat-freak status when he was impatient.

I loved how I did that to him.

"I'm happy to help, naughty girl."

I turned around and swept my veil over my shoulder so it wouldn't be in his way. "There's a hook at the top."

His tone was displeased. "And a shitload of buttons."

I smiled to myself. "Calm down, there's a hidden zipper."

Fingers drew a line where the fabric on my strapless dress stopped, tracing over my skin, and paused at the center to undo the tiny metal hook. Then, the zipper must have been discovered beneath the panel of buttons, because it began to drop, one tooth at a time.

I shivered as his lips floated over my shoulder, ghosting kisses. His hands were inside the back of my dress, pushing the bodice down, and sliding up over my belly. Making me tremble and insane with lust. My fingers fumbled in the small of my back to undo the knot holding my crinoline in place.

The cups were sewn in, so I wasn't wearing a bra, and my sigh of relief was loud when he palmed my breasts. I leaned into him, putting my back against his hardened chest. My eyes fell shut as I waited for his next move. I never knew what kind of sex I'd get with Logan. Did he want to make love tonight? Have a quick, hard fuck? Maybe both?

He enjoyed touching me, moving at an unhurried pace, but my body's response was too strong. I couldn't last much longer, so I shimmied out of the dress and my shoes. A tight noise came from behind.

"I like these." He ran a hand over the swell of my ass, admiring the blue panties I wore that had 'Mrs.' written in tiny rhinestones across the back.

"They were my 'something blue.'"

"Holy shit. It stands up on its own."

He was talking about my dress. "Yeah. No hanger required." The layers of stiff netting and boning supported the dress and kept it upright, defying gravity.

His fingers slipped under my arm and turned me to face him. His gaze traced each centimeter of my naked flesh like it was the first time he was seeing it, and he looked appreciative of the view. The only things I wore were the panties and the veil still attached at the base of my up-do. His expression shifted and grew more intense, mimicking one of a predator. This was the darkest version of Logan I only saw when he was overwhelmed with lust and losing his grip on control.

"I've missed these." Once again, his hands fondled

my breasts, only this time he wasn't gentle. He moved on me urgently, forcing me backward until I slammed into the wall, but he didn't let up. Hands pinched at my already-tight nipples, making me ache while his mouth locked on mine. His tongue thrust deep, and I moaned.

But he stepped back abruptly and the heat of his body vanished, making my eyes fly open in surprise.

"Fuck." He ran a hand through his hair.

"Yes," I said, already breathless. "That's what we should do."

"We'll get to that, don't you worry, but I want to get in the tub."

I glanced at the large, deep Jacuzzi and gave him a dubious look. "You want to take a bath?"

"You mentioned your feet hurt."

They did, and now that I had it off, I was realizing just how heavy the dress had been. A bath with massaging jets and my gorgeous new husband wrapped around me suddenly sounded like the best idea ever.

While he ran the tap, I went to the mirror and began the process of removing my veil. I said it loudly over the rushing water. "There are a thousand pins inside my hair, just so you know."

"Awesome."

Movement from beside the tub stopped me mid-process. Logan was getting undressed and I wasn't about to miss the show. The vest was already open, and the tie hung loose around his neck. Sexy. Then, the shirt was unbuttoned and cufflinks undone. I gasped when he peeled one shoulder out, followed by the other, and dropped all of it to the floor in a heap.

I couldn't stop the grin at how he was breaking his own rules.

"What?" he said. "It's a rental."

"Okay, boss. I can pretend you're not going to pick all that up later because it's bothering you."

He smirked. His hands busied themselves undoing his pants, and it showed off his impressive upper body. All sinewy muscles flexing under his smooth, tan skin. The pants fell off his hips, slid down, and he kicked them away. The black socks were tugged off and added to his pile.

Witnessing Logan in only a pair of black boxer briefs set my body on fire. I freed the comb that the veil was attached to from my hair and, following his lead, I dropped it to the floor.

"Come here." It was a soft request from Logan, not a demand, and I went to him instantly. His hands swept over my skin, greedy to touch what he'd been denied. They plunged beneath the back of my panties, and he gripped a handful of flesh, driving me against his hard body.

"I love you," he whispered between kisses, which grew reckless and frantic, and it was impossible not to match his intensity.

"I love you so much," I answered back, clawing at his underwear.

It was a race to see who could get the other one naked first, but he won, of course. He lifted me up into his arms and stepped into the tub. A moment later he had the faucet shut off and the jets running, both of us sitting in the warm water. My back rested against his chest, while his strong arms held me, and his legs were wrapped around my waist.

There were tiny tugs at my hair. Was he . . . ? I glanced over my shoulder and saw him set the bobby pin on the tile. Then, another. Shit, this man made everything sexy, even something as simple as helping me let my hair down. I grabbed his foot and pulled it into my lap, massaging the sole, and he issued a groan of approval.

We chatted about our morning apart, recapping our favorite moments from the day as he pulled the pins from my hair and I rubbed his tired feet. It wasn't the type of intimacy I thought we'd share the moments after we came into the honeymoon suite, but it was wonderful. I loved the quiet moments with him just as much as the steamy, intense ones.

"I think I got them all," he said. His fingertips drifted down my neck and he rubbed my shoulders as I combed my fingers through my hair, searching for any stragglers.

"Good . . . job," I moaned. His hands were magic.

"What would you say if I told you we should get out so I could fuck my wife senseless?"

"I'd say I like the sound of that."

"Hmm. I thought so."

The jets were shut off and the water gurgled as he lifted the drain stop. I'd barely finished toweling off when he yanked the plush fabric from my hands and threw it to the ground. His expression was pure sexual hunger, only intensified in the candlelight. A gentle shove, and I was sprawled out beneath him on the bed.

"Look at you. All fucking gorgeous and so fucking mine."

My lungs refused to work as he gripped his thick cock and stroked himself, his wedding band the only thing he wore. I couldn't control myself. My fingers flew to my clit, touching myself.

"Oh, shit, Logan. I need you."

He sank down to kneel and placed my knees on his shoulders. My body didn't know how to react. I loved when he went down on me, but I was greedy and impatient. "No, please— God." Then his tongue was inside me, and thought was too difficult. "Yes, *yes.*"

Velvety heat flicked on me, sending sparks radiating out and down my trembling legs. My moans were a mixture of satisfaction and whining, and they grew louder with each of Logan's careful manipulations. Fire seared deep inside, and I bucked off the bed, seizing his head in my hands.

"Make love to me," I cried. Every cell in me was quaking, and I worried I was going to vibrate apart. The only thing that could stop my uncontrollable trembling was if he brought us together.

The bed shifted as he launched to his feet, wiping his mouth with one hand and giving a final stroke to his rock-hard cock. He held himself steady and positioned himself right at the apex of my legs, rubbing the tip in my arousal.

"Green?" he teased.

"So fucking green. Please. *Please.*"

He pushed inside and I wanted to cry at how good

it felt. The stretch the first time he moved in me was like nothing else. My legs tightened around his waist.

"Fuck, Evie. You feel amazing. So wet and so perfect."

My eyes squeezed shut so I could better enjoy the sensations as he slid deep, all the way until I couldn't take him any further. My hands clutched at his chest and he gripped them, linking our fingers together so he could hold my hands flat against the sheets.

His thrusts were slow and calculating. Each one seemed to hit a new spot that was better than the last. His mouth roved over my lips, my neck, and my breasts. I swallowed back a moan as he increased his pace. Spots danced in front of my vision as the orgasm closed in.

"Yellow," I gasped.

I was sure I didn't need to tell him; he knew my body better than I did sometimes. He knew exactly how much I could take, how much I needed.

"Did you . . . hear me?" I said between pants. He hadn't eased up.

His voice and expression were authoritative. "I heard you."

I fought against his hold. He needed to slow his roll or I'd come, which usually made him come. "Fuck. I'm gonna . . . oh, red. Red!"

"No, Evie. You're not allowed." And then his mouth was on mine, sealing me off from asking permission to come. It wasn't a game we played while I'd imposed the rule, and with what he was doing to me, I'd forgotten all about it.

I turned my head away from him and my voice shook as I demanded it. "I need permission."

"For what?" He whispered it in my ear, his tone coy.

"Permission to come."

He sucked on the tender spot of my neck, just below my ear. He drove into me. This wasn't lovemaking. He was owning my body now, and I lifted my hips up off the mattress, eager to meet him.

"Okay, Mrs. Stone. You have my permission to come."

I let out a cry, or maybe a scream as it began. Sparks of pleasure burst, lifting me higher and higher, until I fell over the crest of bliss. My muscles tightened and strained against the sensations rolling through me. As the intensity of the orgasm began to fade, warmth washed from the tips of my toes upward.

"Fuck. Oh, fuck." Logan's curse words signaled the trigger had been pulled on his release. His right hand abandoned mine, and scooped beneath my neck, cradling my head. "Open your eyes."

His damp forehead rested against mine and I followed his command. *Oh my God.* His fascinating eyes stared down into my soul as he shuddered. He came hard, and loudly. Every desperate gasp for breath was for me. The throbbing of his body inside mine . . . I'd never get enough of this. My connection to him was so strong, nothing could break it.

His skin, still damp from the bath, or perhaps slick with sweat, stuck to mine, but I didn't care. For a long while we lay on the bed kissing and touching, enjoying each other.

"Want to make a deal?" I whispered.

"I'm listening."

"You blow out all these candles and let me lie here, and I'll blow you when you're done."

He twisted his mouth into a knowing smile. "Right. I'm sure you won't be fast asleep when I get back here."

I put my hand on his jaw, brushing my thumb over his lips. "I didn't say when *specifically* I'd blow you."

"New rule, then. Promised oral sex must be delivered in a timely fashion."

I giggled. "No more rules, Logan."

He rose up on an elbow and brushed a lock of my hair out of my eyes, his face going serious. "One more rule. We say 'I love you' every night before we fall asleep."

It was something we already did, so I had no problem defining it this way. "Absolutely."

"Don't go breaking it, rule breaker." He faked a strict, harsh look.

"Never, boss. I love you."

"I love you too, Evie." He pressed his lips to mine in a kiss full of passion. "More than you can even imagine."

And since I knew how much I loved him, I could imagine a lot.

CONTINUE READING WITH

THREE LITTLE MISTAKES

&

THREE DIRTY SECRETS

&

THREE SWEET NOTHINGS

TABLE *for* TWO

THE BLINDFOLD CLUB
NOVELLA 5.5

Chapter ONE

JULIUS

I was buying suits like girls bought gallons of ice cream to cheer them up. It was getting really fucking expensive, but at least I could afford it.

Courtney Crawford was going on a date. Tonight. Her first official date since her divorce six months ago, and it was killing me. I'd bought my first suit after I got her text about it last week. The gray fabric was so dark, it was almost black, and it matched my shitty mood. I also got a maroon silk tie and pocket square that had small white polka dots. It looked good, like I had money and style.

I ordered the second suit when she called me on Tuesday, wanting advice on where she should go if the guy asked for ideas. Nowhere, I wanted to say. Go out with me instead. Fuck. If I'd known she was ready, maybe I would have done something about it.

Who was I kidding? We were friends, and I didn't want to fuck that up.

I'd watched her with another guy for the last seven years. I'd stood up at her and Tariq's wedding because he was my boy and had asked me to. I didn't know how the hell to say no. Didn't want him figuring out I was in love with his girl and have him take her away from me.

I told myself it was cool. Courtney and I could just be

friends. I'd rather have that, than nothing at all.

But then he'd started cheating on her.

Wait, fuck that. He'd always been cheating on her. She knew about it when we'd been at Ohio State. He said it was a one-time fuck-up. It'd never happen when she was his wife. Tariq was a beast on the football field and an asshole off it, but he was smart enough to know he needed to lock Courtney down.

The front door of the shop chimed when I pushed it open, and I marched toward the counter in the back. The place was dead, but it was three o'clock on a Friday. The only man I saw working didn't look familiar, and it added to my irritation. Two years ago, I owned one suit, which I never wore and barely fit into. Now, I had a closet full of them, all tailored to the last motherfucking detail, and a specific guy I liked when I shopped here.

"Where's Maurice?" I asked.

The guy behind the register was pale, almost like he'd never been outside. His nametag said 'Brandon' but maybe it was really Casper. He stared up at me and his Adam's apple bobbed as he swallowed hard. I got that a lot. I was a big motherfucker.

"He's out today," Casper said. "Can I help you with something?"

"I got a call telling me my suit's ready."

"Your name?"

"Julius King."

He nodded, disappeared into the back, and reappeared holding the top of the hanger sticking out of the black garment bag.

I took it from him. "I gotta check the fit."

"Of course. Please let me know if you need anything." He motioned toward the fitting rooms.

Don't think about Courtney. I stripped out of my jeans and t-shirt, and pulled on the suit pants. Don't think about the lucky fucker who'd been set up on the blind date with her. I shoved my arms through the crisp black dress shirt that was also custom-made. Don't think about how Kyle betrayed you, arranging the whole GD thing. He was supposed to be my friend. The only one who knew how I felt about Courtney, and then he went and fucking set her up with someone else.

Asshole. I hadn't texted him back since I found out. I was almost thirty, but not too old to give his ass the silent treatment.

I buttoned the shirt, pulled the jacket off the hanger, and put it on. The fit was good. The suit was a deep purple, and looked classy without being stuffy. I stepped out of the room and went to the full-length mirror, where Casper lurked.

His eyes widened. "Wow. Looks great."

"Thanks, man."

I stared at my reflection. I should have felt good. My linebacker build was physically impressive, and the expensive clothes made me seem professional. I looked powerful, and when I scowled, people nearly shit themselves. But I'd learned a while back how a smile got me a hell of a lot further. I liked smiling better, anyway.

Not today. My frown made Casper go five shades whiter.

"How does it feel?" he asked, nervous. "Is there something wrong with the fit?"

"Nah." I forced the scowl away. "Bad day, is all."

Casper nodded. "Hey, at least it's Friday."

Except Friday was the beginning of my 'work week,' not the end of it. And it was Friday, the day she was going out with him. For once, I wasn't looking forward to going to my club. Being around all the sex was going to make me think about Court and if she was going to fuck her date tonight if things went well.

"I'm gonna wear it out," I said. "Is that cool?"

The tags were already gone, removed before the tailoring, and I'd worn the right pair of shoes into the store. I figured I'd go straight from the shop to the club, and get some shit sorted out before opening tonight. Anything to keep my mind off her.

"Of course, sir," Casper said. "You're all set. Have a nice night."

Yeah, that was real fucking doubtful.

Chapter TWO

JULIUS

I sat at my desk and eyeballed the bottle of bourbon. Kyle had given it to me as a birthday present. It was some classy shit, or so he said, but I didn't like it. I stuck it in my office to make me look good. Even though this place was a blindfold club, looks mattered.

My club was my kingdom. My leather desk chair was so big, some of the girls called it my throne, and when I was in it, I could see every inch of the place through the monitors. Nothing went down in the rooms without me knowing about it.

Was it too early to start drinking?

Some of my staff were already in the building, but the girls wouldn't show up for another few hours.

I checked my phone. Court hadn't texted me. She hadn't sent out an SOS asking for help bailing on her date, which had started thirty minutes ago. Plenty of time for her to sneak away to the bathroom and tell me how awful the guy was . . . but she hadn't. Fuck, it meant the date was going well.

Panic was too big a word, but it was like ants were crawling on me. I'd waited too long. I was gonna miss my window, and wasn't going to be lucky enough to get another chance with her. I had to fucking do something.

When I called her, it went right to voicemail. I thumbed out a text instead of leaving a message.

> Me: Need to talk. It's important.

Minutes dragged by. The text said it'd been delivered, but not read. I set the phone down, covered my fist with my other hand, and cracked my knuckles all at the same time. I pictured her at a fancy-ass restaurant, sitting across the table from some asshole attorney, which the guy had to be since all of Kyle's friends were lawyers, and she'd be smiling her smile that made me forget how to speak words. I should be that guy. That smile was for me.

Fuck. If I couldn't get in touch with her, maybe I could get the guy on the phone. Kyle owed me.

> Me: The bourbon you gave me tastes like shit.

A meme jumped on the screen. "New phone, who dis?" The three dots blinked by as Kyle continued typing.

> Kyle: Fuck you. I don't hear from you all week, and that's what you open with?

> Me: I need dude's name and number.

> Kyle: Sorry, can't give it to you.

> Me: U R an asshole.

> Kyle: True.

It was still early. Unless she was out in the suburbs, I could ambush her date and make it back to the club before it opened. Traffic would have to cooperate. Didn't happen much in Chicago, but a brother could hope.

Whatever. Focus.

> Me: Name and number. Or you call him.
>
> Kyle: And tell him what?
>
> Me: Setting them up was a mistake.
>
> Kyle: Was it? Sounds like you finally want to make your move.

I stabbed my finger at the phone so hard, I was lucky it didn't break.

> Me: ASSHOLE.
>
> Kyle: Yeah, we established that. If it helps, this thing wasn't my idea. Going into a movie. Text me later.

Was he shitting me?

> Me: WTF?

There was no response.

> Me: Hope your dick falls off.

The bastard didn't answer me. I stared at the bottle of nasty-ass liquor and got angry as fuck. What the hell was I going to do?

I'm a powerful guy. Connected to everyone, and treated like goddamn royalty. The superintendent of the Chicago PD was a client, and I cooperated with the FBI when some big-time john came through my doors. I could pull favors in an emergency. One phone call and I'd have most of the city out looking for Courtney Crawford.

Goddammit. That would be some crazy-ass shit, right there.

Instead, as much as it'd fucking suck, I'd sit here and wait for her to answer my message. I'd been through worse nights at the club. I'd tussled with another bouncer here once, and broken a client's jaw when he strangled one of my girls half-to-death. I didn't like fighting. Didn't like the feeling of my fists pounding against something soft and warm, and knowing I was causing pain. No judgment of the guys who came to the club to get off like that, but I liked using my hands to give pleasure.

"Julius," a male voice echoed through my earpiece. It was Deiondre, my newest security guy. "Some girl's at the front. You got an audition tonight?"

Not that I knew about, but sometimes a girl I was recruiting showed up without scheduling. I focused on the screen at the main entrance, enlarging it so I—

It felt like I'd been smacked in the center of my chest with a football helmet.

What the fuck?

No idea what Courtney was doing here. Only thing I knew was Kyle McCreary was a motherfucking dead man.

Courtney looked nervous as hell, and I wasn't too proud to admit I was scared shitless. She didn't know what I did. I fed her the same line of bullshit everyone else got, that the blindfold club was an exclusive, members only, wine club.

I'd been grandfathered in with the lie, thanks to her husband Tariq. I wasn't embarrassed about the business I ran. Why the fuck should I be? Everyone who walked through the door wanted to be here, especially my girls. I kept them safe, gave them a classy place to do their business, and we all made truckloads of cash.

But I couldn't go back on the lie once it'd been told. Court would have questions, and one of them would be if her husband had ever visited. I'd been trapped. Tariq and I had played football together at Ohio State, and he was real fucking quick to remind me *"Bros before hoes."* The longer it went on, the deeper my hole got.

Every time Tariq showed up at my club, cheated on his wife, and I didn't say a fucking thing to her, it was like I was the bigger bastard. My betrayal stung more.

"She's asking about you," Deiondre said. "You want me to send her up?"

Fuck, no! I launched to my feet. "I'll come down. Don't say nothing to her."

I took the stairs down, two steps at a time. All the doors in the main hallway were open and the cleaning people were busy inside the client rooms, prepping for the night. A war drum pounded in my chest, harder than the moments in the tunnel before a big football game. How much had Kyle told her?

Shit, what if this was the end of me and her, before we even got going?

No. I wouldn't let that happen. I yanked the door open to the entry checkpoint and put my hands on the doorframe, blocking the inside of the club from view.

Seven years ago, Court had been a cheerleader at Ohio State. She was five-foot-nothing and maybe a buck-ten, as my Grampa would say. Tiny. Blonde, white, and so fucking pretty she'd been used in a bunch of the marketing material for OSU's football program.

And she just got better looking as the years went by. First time I'd seen her when Tariq brought them to Chicago, she'd cut her long hair short and gone darker. Still blonde, but more natural looking. It made her eyes bluer and brighter. Made her look sexier, which I didn't think was possible.

I couldn't stop my gaze as it slid down her tight body. Was she wearing leather pants? Fuck me, the girl was a dime whatever she had on, but the loose, draping shirt she wore was mean. It covered her perfect ass from view, and I needed to see it in those pants she'd poured herself into.

When Court's gaze landed on me, a smile broke out, and wires crossed in my brain. She didn't look pissed . . . she looked relieved. What the fuck? Maybe Kyle hadn't told her anything. Maybe she'd gotten the address somehow and still thought this place was legit.

I dug my fingers into the wood frame of the door where she couldn't see my grip, and tried to sound normal. "Courtney? What're you doing here?"

She stared at my suit and blinked. Was the color throwing her off? Her big blue eyes shifted to look up at my face. "You wanted to talk." She took a step forward. Even in heels, she was a foot shorter than me. "You said it was important."

I worked my fingers deeper between the wood. If I went after it, I'd separate the jam from the wall. "Yeah, but how'd—"

Her voice was casual and steady. "I know what you do. I've known about this place for months, Julius." She glanced at Deiondre, then back to me. "Can we go inside?"

The door frame splintered and cracked in my hand, making her jolt. She'd known . . . *for months*? I brought my hands down, jamming them in my pockets as I turned to let her through the doorway. My brain chugged along, trying to keep up.

Courtney was dressed to go out, but she was alone.

"Did I fuck up your date?" I asked.

Her faint smile made my confusion worse. "No."

As she walked past, I got a hit of her perfume. Just a hint of her scent had me swallowing hard. Did this girl have any idea what she did to me? I pulled the handle closed, putting a door between us and Deiondre.

Courtney took in her surroundings. The narrow room had fancy couches on one side and a bar on the other, which was currently dark. When we were open, I staffed one guy behind it. He made sure the clients had whatever they wanted before their appointments, or if it was a walk-in, they had to hang out in this room while I evaluated their membership application and went over the rules.

"I got questions," I said. A fuck-ton of questions.

She nodded, but stared at the floor instead of looking at me. "I do, too. Like, if you had ruined my date... would you be glad?"

Trap, my brain warned. There were way bigger things to talk about right now. Worry squeezed my voice. "What do you know about my club?"

"You don't sell wine."

I sucked down a breath and my shoulders lifted. My chest was tight. "Yeah? What do I sell?"

Finally, she looked at me and licked her lips. She did that shit when she was nervous, and had no fucking clue how much it turned me on. Her mouth was sexy as hell. She was so quiet, it was almost a whisper and I couldn't tell if she was judging me. "You sell women."

My pulse kicked up another notch. "Nah, not exactly."

Her eyes went big and she looked confused. "Then, you tell me, because I heard you—"

"I sell an experience."

Her lush lips rounded into an '*oh*.' The sudden urge to grab her and slam my mouth over hers was fierce, but I kept my motherfucking hands in my pockets. She hesitated, but the look in her eyes... what was that? Interest?

"An experience," she repeated, "with beautiful women, who are naked, blindfolded and bound."

Shit, she really did know. "Who told you?" I asked.

It wouldn't be Tariq. Their divorce was messy, and... fuck me. It couldn't have been Kyle either. Besides him saying he wouldn't tell her, he'd been my attorney, too. That was privileged info.

She peered up at me like I was fascinating, not disgusting. How was that fucking possible? My heart roared along, like a stupid girl skipping through flowers. Courtney was my best friend. Having her know this and not judge me was fucking *huge*.

"There's a guy who plays offense for the Bears. He came here last year with his wife, and . . ." She shrugged. "Players' wives talk."

I staggered back a step, taking in the info I hadn't seen coming. As a businessman, I was glad she hadn't said the client's name. We didn't use them in the club, since the whole point of the blindfolds was to keep identities a secret.

Courtney tucked a lock of her hair behind her ear. "She was, uh . . . complimentary of your place."

"I gotta sit down." I plodded over to the nearest couch, dropped into it, and set my forehead in my hand. Holy shit. No point dancing around it. "Whatcha think when you found out?"

Her heels tapped across the floor, and she sank slowly down onto the other side of the couch. "I was worried. I mean, what you're doing isn't legal."

"I'm fine," I said, rubbing my forehead with my fingertips. "I ain't going anywhere." Not to prison, because I had an airtight arrangement with the Feds.

"Right after I found out, you met Kyle and you said he helped you with stuff. So, I suspect he advised you how to operate without . . ." she searched for the right thing to say, "getting into trouble."

I let out a breath. I was glad to come clean on one secret, but couldn't tell her the whole truth. If my deal with the FBI collapsed, it wasn't just my neck, it was every one of my employees' too, and that was a big deal for me.

"Something like that." I straightened and turned to her. "You mad at me for not telling you?"

"No. I figured you would when you were ready." She smiled softly. "But . . . I got impatient. You know I fucking suck at keeping secrets."

It was true. How had she gone months without telling me she knew about my club?

"And as long as we're talking about secrets . . ." Her breathing picked up and her face flushed.

Fuck. This had to be about Tariq. Did she know he'd been a regular until their divorce? Until I'd finally stopped being a stupid fucking idiot, picked her over him, and threw Tariq's ass out of my club?

"I didn't have a date tonight." She licked her lips nervously. "I thought maybe you'd tell me *everything* when you were ready."

My heart stopped skipping and slammed into a brick wall. "What?"

She lifted up and scooted closer to me. The nearness of her tripped proximity alarms in my head, and I tensed to keep myself from leaning into her. She swallowed a breath. "I know our situation's complicated. We're friends, and I was with Tariq. I get why you're nervous."

I played at being casual. "Who's nervous?"

Courtney moved again, inching her way toward me, and I stayed glued to the couch cushions. I liked this a lot. The building could be on fire, but I wasn't fucking moving.

What was she getting at, though?

"If you didn't have a date tonight, why'd you tell me you did?" And all that shit with Kyle—what was that about?

She slid until she was right beside me. Her knee, wrapped in that sleek leather, was up against my thigh. Courtney pressed her lips together, and her gaze dropped to my chest. I didn't like seeing her anxious, but couldn't think of a damn thing to say to make her more comfortable.

"I was hoping you'd tell me not to go."

"Fuck, Courtney." Sitting beside her was like being on a roller coaster. It flipped my stomach, but in the best kind of way. "I should of. I wanted to, but I thought it'd fuck things up between us." I couldn't fight the urge any longer and leaned close, right up to the edge of the friend zone, and then pushed passed it. "You want . . . more?"

I'll give you everything I've got, just say the word, girl.

She stared at me like she was torn, but between what? Nerves? Worry about things changing? Her eyebrows came together. "Yeah, I do, but—" she glanced around the room, "—I need to know what *you* do here."

My brain was still stuck on her answer and I couldn't follow. "I run the club."

"What I mean is, I'm not going to get into anything with you if I have to . . . share." Her expression went hard. "I already shared my man once, and it's definitely not my thing."

Now I got it. "I don't fuck my girls. I don't even touch 'em." She gave me some side-eye, but I laughed. "For real. I'm their boss."

I stopped before I said the girls were like my sisters, because that always sounded creepy as fuck, but it was the only way to explain how I felt. I cared about every one of my employees like we were a twisted, messed up family. And you see someone naked enough times, it stops being weird and becomes your version of normal.

Same for watching them fuck on the security footage.

Still didn't look like she believed me. "What happens at an audition?" she asked.

I'd changed some things when I took over. Originally at an audition, the girl got naked and went down on the owner. For Joseph, that wasn't just about her proving herself, it was to give him power. I wasn't into any of that.

"The girl gets naked," I said quickly.

Court frowned. "That's it?"

It wasn't. I took them into a room and . . . "I watch her get herself off."

Her face went blank. "Oh."

"I didn't tell you about this place, I know. But you gotta believe I ain't lying about this, Court."

"Okay," she said with a tight voice. "How about you give me a tour then?"

Chapter
THREE

COURTNEY

Julius King was unexpected. He was huge with an intimidating build, yet he was the nicest, sweetest guy I knew. Back in college, he'd been surprisingly fast on the football field. After we graduated, he'd gone into security for the club . . . only to end up owning the place.

Even his deep purple suit and black dress shirt was unexpected. I hadn't seen him dressed in a suit since the tux he'd worn at my wedding. This one fit much better, and the eggplant color looked beautiful on him. He was like modern-day royalty as he stood from the couch and gestured toward the other door in the room, the one which led further inside his club.

My best friend owned a brothel. I'd known for months, but seeing really was believing, and it was hard to wrap my head around it.

He hadn't changed much physically from the guy I'd met at a house party Tariq had taken me to after a football game our junior year. Julius had shaved his head after graduation and kept the look. He was thick with bulky muscle. His bicep was probably bigger than my thigh, and the weekend after my divorce had been finalized, I'd had two glasses of wine and wondered what it'd be like to have his powerful arms around me.

The thought made me shiver. It felt wrong to like the idea so much because he'd been my friend for years, but it also felt . . . completely right. On paper, we shouldn't click. We were opposites in every way, literally black and white, but instead we fit together perfectly.

And once the idea of us moving from friends into something more was in my mind, I couldn't stop thinking about him.

I wasn't sure how long he'd had feelings for me. If it was before I'd come to Chicago, he'd done a damn good job of hiding it, but the more time we spent together, the more obvious it became. He got braver over the last few months, and I did everything I could to encourage him.

But I wasn't laying it down hard enough, I guess. My eagerness reached a critical turning point when my sister asked if she could set me up with a guy from her gym. I knew what I wanted, and I was fairly confident it was the same thing Julius did, but I also didn't want to be ninety years old when he finally made his move.

And it'd been months since I'd had sex with anything that wasn't battery operated. Julius was attractive and worked at a club surrounded by beautiful women who sold their bodies for money, which he had plenty of. Times were desperate. I wasn't going to lose him before I'd even gotten him.

My legs were jelly as I stood from the couch. I believed in what I was doing, but that didn't mean it was easy, and I could not get a handle on my nerves. They rattled in my chest, vibrating me from the inside out.

His eyes were jet black and filled with concern, but I couldn't tell if it was for me or for himself. Was he worried I'd judge him? The concept of him running a brothel took some getting used to, but I'd done it. There were legal jobs he could have had that were worse than this. Above all, I trusted he knew what he was doing.

"I've never given a tour before," Julius said. "How much do you want to see?"

My body temperature rose and made my weak knees worse. I'd had fantasies about this place. All of them included the man before me. He said he didn't touch the women, but did he live this lifestyle? Would he tie me up or blindfold me if I asked him to?

I could barely choke the words out over my excitement. "All of it. Walk me through what you do."

He drew in an unsure breath. "This room is where a client hangs out before his appointment."

"His?" I repeated. Cordell and his wife had played together, living out their mutual fantasy of a threesome, but . . . "You only take men?"

"Nah, we take women and couples too, but ninety-nine percent of the members are guys." He strode to the door, but hesitated before opening it for me. "You sure you're cool with this? Shit's gonna get real."

It was like he'd lit a firecracker and tossed it inside me. I bit down on my bottom lip and nodded quickly. I was dying to see more. Would the blindfold club match the sexy images I'd painted in my mind?

He tugged the door open.

The hallway, like the holding room we'd just come from, was dim. Black walls, broken up by open doorways on both sides. Security lighting in the corners was bright enough to see, but it made the long hallway feel ominous.

"I don't have the lights on since we're not open yet," Julius said.

"Oh." It was all I could think to say.

I shuffled forward a few feet and glanced into the room to my left. It looked like the living area of an elegant hotel suite. There was a big screen television mounted on the wall, a couch, and what seemed to be a wet bar area. That wasn't what I expected at all. No bed?

"We got a few client rooms," he said. "Overflow if we book two at the same time. We hold the guy here until his girl's ready."

Oh. A tingle crept along my skin as I glanced to my right. There was a brass number two on the door, and my gaze swept further inside. This room was lit by a glowing crystal chandelier, and the prisms cast subtle rainbows on the wall. It was the only color. Everything, including the table in the center of the space, was black except for the white wingback chair in a back corner.

He didn't tell me it was okay to go inside the room, but I did it anyway. The table was like a large cabinet with a black leather cushion top.

"This is where it happens?" My voice was breathless.

"Yeah."

I pictured getting on the table, and shuddered with unexpected pleasure at the mental image. "How does it work?"

Julius shuffled a few feet into the room. "The sales assistant helps the girl get blindfolded and strapped down, and waits for the client to come in."

I paused. "Sales assistant?"

"Another girl. She'll negotiate the price."

I stared at the empty wingback chair. "Does she stay during?"

"Nah, she leaves when a deal's done."

"Is that . . . safe? Leaving the girl alone with the guy?"

Something flickered through his expression. Was he shy all of a sudden? "It's safe. We got cameras and I'm watching in my office."

I felt stupid for not thinking of that, but then my eyes widened. "Holy shit, Julius. You *watch*? What's that like?" I couldn't stop the surprised smile from rushing across my face. "Is it sexy?"

He shook his head. "It's work." He rubbed a hand on the back of his neck, showing off his hulking form. "And it's probably gonna give me an ulcer. A lot of the guys, they're nothing to worry about. All they want is to fuck a hot girl. But I always gotta watch for that one asshole who wants to push things. The motherfucker who goes too far."

His uncharacteristically dark look made me think it had happened before.

My gaze went back to the table as I struggled to find a change in topic. He'd said the girl was tied down, but—"Where are the straps?"

"Top drawer."

It felt like he was cool with me peeking. I grabbed the silver knob and slid the drawer open. Swaths of black ribbon were coiled neatly inside, and beside them, stacks of black blindfolds wrapped in clear plastic.

There were three other drawers beneath this one. It didn't make a sound as I closed it, and neither did the next one I opened. My breath stalled in my lungs. The drawer was partitioned, and each section held a different item. Vibrators. Dildos. Plugs.

"That one's for pleasure." Julius's deep voice broke the quiet in the room.

As I stared down at the toys, I could feel his gaze on me, and I grew hot. The air in the room thickened and became hard to breathe.

The next drawer down was also partitioned. Paddles. Riding crops. Nipple clamps. A looped item I suspected was a whip.

"That drawer's for pain."

There was something buried in his tone, and I knew him well enough to recognize it. He didn't care for this drawer, which was interesting. I peered at it with fascination, but also trepidation. I'd been a vanilla girl most of my life, but had always been curious, and Tariq's betrayal was a catalyst to broadening my sex life.

It shouldn't have been surprising the 'pain' drawer made Julius uneasy. The guy was the sweetest thing ever. He looked intimidating, but he had a gentle heart. Yet, he ran a BDSM sex club. Wasn't this drawer a huge part of that?

I closed it and opened the final drawer, moving slowly because my body was sluggish with lust. There were strap-on harnesses. A wand with feathers at the end, and other things I didn't recognize.

"That drawer is for both."

My tone was skeptical. "Feathers can cause pain?"

"You got ticklish feet, Court. Think about if you couldn't move or get away."

Oh, God. He was right. That'd be torture. My gaze landed on the black woven handle. I gestured toward it. "Can I—?"

He looked exactly how I felt. Tense with desire, but trying not to show it. His head bobbed in a single nod.

I slipped my hand around the handle of the flogger and pulled it slowly from the drawer. The long leather tails dangled until I circled my fist around them and dragged the bunch through my closed hand. I could only see this tool slapping against skin and causing pain. "How is this one both?"

He sucked in a deep breath. Maybe he was struggling to breathe the thick air as much as I was. "When used right, it can feel good."

He said it with enough confidence, it sounded like he was talking from experience. Shit, I was going to burn up from the inside. The fire was so intense, it seared away my vocal cords and kept me from asking him to show me right now.

Instead, I tucked the flogger back neatly where I'd found it, shut the drawer and straightened. My pulse roared in my body, thumping the hardest between my legs. It pounded out an ache I wanted Julius to satisfy, but I struggled with how to get what I needed.

The first year here in Chicago had been brutal. The other football wives were nice enough, but Tariq had a not-great reputation, which followed him off the field and became mine by association. Julius was the only real friend I had, and I'd leaned on him hard when I discovered Tariq's cheating. He'd helped me get through the divorce, which had driven a wedge between the men who'd played ball together in college. I felt bad their friendship ended, but secretly I was thrilled Julius had chosen to stick by my side.

I laid my nervous hands on the cushioned top of the table and stared at my splayed fingers, searching for courage. I didn't want to screw up what we had, but couldn't fight my feelings any longer. I longed for him with every shallow breath I took.

I hoisted myself up, turning around to sit with my legs dangling over the side.

Alarm coasted through Julius's handsome face. "What're you doing?"

"I want to see what it's like," I said in a rush.

His concern shifted to confusion, and in a few steps, he was right in front of me. "C'mon, don't play like that."

Only his statement was filled with cautious hope. When he set one of his large hands on my shoulder to help me down, it was the connection we needed. It turned the key in the lock on my desire, and set it tumbling free.

I reached for him, grasping his face in my hands, and pulled him down into my kiss.

Chapter FOUR

COURTNEY

I hadn't kissed another man in seven years, and bringing my lips to Julius's was fireworks. It was everything I'd hoped it be, and then some. My fingers bristled against the rough ends of the whiskers darkening his defined jaw when I pulled him closer. He had on cologne or some type of woodsy scent that smelled amazing.

His soft lips pressed to mine, stunned at first, and then the intensity of the moment hit us with its full force. I was kissing Julius King . . . and he was kissing me.

Oh my God, how he was kissing me.

His mouth was passionate and commanding. His hot tongue moved past my lips, seeking mine, and its sexy, slow movement was the same as if he'd stroked his hands between my thighs. I felt it along every nerve ending in my body.

His hands seized my waist and hauled me to the edge of the table, causing me to wrap my legs around his hips. We were wild. Out of control with lust. I'd worried about making the wrong move, but this felt so goddamn right, I was mad I waited so long.

The softest of moans slipped from me as his kiss intensified another layer. The ache for him grew like an unpredictable tornado and left me spinning. I clung to him, holding on for dear life. Would I ever be able to let go?

It was easily the most passionate kiss of my life, and I let out a hushed cry of displeasure when he ended it. His hands still circled my waist and he didn't go far. His warm forehead rested against mine, his eyes closed, and for a long moment we stayed like that, working to get our breathing back under control.

"Jesus," he whispered.

His single stunned word announced how much this kiss meant to him, and it was powerful. It had meant *so* much to me. I slid my hands down his neck until I had my palms flat against his broad, hard chest.

"Maybe you should," I said between two gulps of air, "shut the door."

His eyes popped open, but he seemed foggy. "What?"

If I said it fast, I could get through it before I lost the courage. "I want to see what it's like for the girl on the table, and you said she's naked."

My statement literally knocked him back, and I'd never seen my friend look more surprised. Part of him liked this idea a lot, but the other part was conflicted. He wiped a hand over the smooth dome of his head, considering how to respond. As words failed him, a stone of embarrassment grew to the size of a boulder in my stomach.

"You don't want to?" I whispered.

"No, I do," he said instantly. "Fuck, you have no idea how much I want to." He threw a hand toward the table. "But like this? The first time we . . ." His posture stiffened. "The table you're sitting on, it ain't right for that. It isn't *special* enough for you."

I softened, understanding what he meant, but this was important. I needed him to see I was okay with what this club was. Yet, I felt like I was losing him. "You said this place was an experience." I slicked my sweaty palms down over my leather-clad thighs. "We don't have to have sex, we could do other . . . stuff."

He blinked slowly. "What're you offering?"

His question sparked an idea. "Isn't that how it starts here? With negotiations?" I dragged a seductive smile across my lips. "I want this. What do you want? What can I give you to make this happen?"

He let out a half of a laugh, making a sound like I was crazy, and grinned. It froze on his face as he grew serious. "A date."

"A date?" I repeated, not expecting such a simple demand.

"Yeah, a real fucking date at some fancy restaurant, where you let me pay for everything."

A laugh welled up inside me. "Now I'm concerned for your business, because you don't seem to get how negotiating works. You're supposed to ask for stuff I *don't* want."

One long stride and he was back at the edge of the table, his face only inches from mine. His voice was commanding. "You're gonna wear that red dress you wore to your sister's thing when she got engaged."

My mouth went dry. I'd met Julius, Kyle and his girlfriend Ruby for drinks after my sister's engagement party two weeks ago. The red dress was short and had a plunging neckline. I'd bought it to make myself feel better. Tariq's adultery wasn't my fault. It wasn't on me. I was almost thirty, but I still looked damn good, and the dress was a reminder I could be sexy.

I could be . . . wanted.

"After dinner," Julius continued, his tone confident, "you're gonna come back to my place and stay the night. I'm not talking about fucking. I want you in my bed. I want to wake up next to you. You asked what I want, and that's it."

I nearly melted down the side of the table, not just from his words, but the way he set his powerful, dark hands gently on my knees and slid them up my thighs. His touch was electricity, sparking across my skin.

"Deal?" he asked.

I choked out the terms in an eager voice. "You show me what it's like on this table, and I'll give you a date and wear the red dress." I set my hands on top of his and curled my fingers around them, inching his hold up onto my waist. "I'll spend the night in your bed."

I was sure we'd do a heck of a lot more than just sleep, but it was sexy to leave the promise unspoken. He tipped his head down and sealed his lips over mine. This kiss was slow, but just as intense as the last one, and I tightened my grip on his.

He didn't confirm the deal with words. Instead, when the kiss was over, he went to the door and pushed it closed. He lingered, facing the wall with his broad back to me, and he put his hand on a hip.

"Deiondre," he said. "I'm in room two and taking out my earpiece. Nobody knocks on the door unless it's really fucking important, got it?"

Whatever answer he received, it seemed to satisfy him. Julius turned to face me, and as he peeled off his suit coat, he strode toward the white chair. The coat was folded neatly and set on the cushion. He unhooked the earpiece with spiraled cord, tugged the small battery pack attached to his waist, and set the communication system down on top of the coat.

A tremble of excitement began at my ankles and worked its way up to my knees as he locked his gaze on me and began to unbutton the cuffs of his black dress shirt. He rolled his sleeves back to the elbow, showing off his strong forearms. His skin was darker than Tariq's, and much more beautiful. I couldn't wait to see more of Julius.

"You gonna get naked?" he teased, but again, there was a hidden edge, like he was worried I was going to change my mind. "Want my help?" he asked lightly.

I wasn't normally shy, but I was nervous having him out of reach. "Do you want to take my clothes off?"

"It's not about me right now. It's whatever you want."

I slid down off the table to stand beside it. "Okay. I want you to do it."

The room was charged with energy and my body was a live wire. His eyes hooded at my request, and he complied, dipping his fingers under the hem of my top and slowly working it up. Our gazes were fixed on each other, broken only for a second as he tugged the shirt over my head, and dropped it silently to the floor.

His Adam's apple bobbed with a thick swallow.

I stood absolutely still as his fingers landed at the button of my pants and undid it. He inched my zipper down, but his eyes never strayed from mine. It was like he found my eyes more interesting than the skin he was revealing.

I gasped when he put his hands under my arms and lifted, seating me on the table. Then, he slipped off my heels and tugged my pants off, one leg at a time. My chest rose and fell with my hurried breath, and then quit moving altogether as his hands crept along my body, his fingertips searching for the hooks at the back of my bra.

His mouth was damp and warm against the side of my neck, planting kisses there as tension released from the band and my bra came undone. Oh, shit. This was the moment of no return. I was about to be topless.

He must have sensed my hesitation. "Okay?"

I grabbed him by the back of the neck and moved his head toward mine until our mouths could meet. I was more than okay, I'd just needed a moment to acknowledge the threshold we were going to cross. As we kissed, I pulled my bra free from my body and added it to the pile of clothes on the floor.

His hands roamed over my bare back and goosebumps burst on my skin. My nipples tightened into points under the cool air and the anticipation of his hands touching me.

But he didn't.

At least, not on my breasts. He turned me on the

tabletop and eased me down onto my back, his dark brown eyes intently watching me. The leather was smooth and cold, and every muscle in me tensed. I'd negotiated for this, but anxiety crept in. It grew larger as his gaze finally broke from mine and he pulled open the top drawer.

My hands were balled into fists at my sides, and I bit down on my bottom lip. Should I take off my panties while he was busy getting the straps ready? I couldn't make myself move. Watching him was too distracting.

Plastic crinkled as he pulled out the black blindfold. He held onto it, hesitating, and my body took over. I tugged the blindfold from his hold, slipped the straps behind my head, and pulled the shade down over my eyes.

In the darkness, I calmed almost instantly. The blindfold covered my nerves, so all I was left with was so much excitement, I worried I'd burst. His fingers gently wrapped around one of my wrists and urged it up over my head.

"If you wanna stop, just tell me," he said.

I didn't want him to stop . . . in fact, I couldn't wait to get started. Anticipation thundered through my bloodstream, heating me to a million degrees.

The scratchy sound of Velcro coming together filled my ears as he closed the first restraint, and then he took my other wrist and did the same. I startled as his unexpected fingers curled around the sides of my thong and drew the scrap of fabric down my legs.

Blindfolded, bound, and now naked, I was more physically vulnerable than I'd ever been, but Julius had already seen me at my most emotionally. He'd been there for me, and so showing him this version was . . . easy. It only strengthened my connection to him.

And speaking of connection—was he going to touch me? After he'd removed my panties, his hands were gone. It didn't sound like he was moving. He was standing beside the table, just breathing.

"What are you doing?" I asked softly.

"Looking at you." God, his voice was like velvet. "Jesus, Courtney. You're so fucking beautiful."

It punched a sigh from my lungs. The ache for him pulsed incessantly in every cell of my body. "Are you going to touch me?"

"You better fucking believe it." His fingertips trailed over my cheekbone, just below the edge of the blindfold. It was his warning so I didn't startle when his lips settled on mine. This kiss was seductive, even though seduction was unnecessary. Even if I wasn't tied down, I'd do whatever he wanted.

He used one fingertip to draw a line over my lips, tracing down my chin and along my neck. Its slow path forced more goosebumps to pebble on my flesh. It was the only place we were connected, but I felt his power *everywhere*.

"You like it?" he asked.

His touch, or being under his control? The answer was a strong *yes* to either. I pressed my lips into a thin line and nodded quickly. I had to squeeze my knees together against the sensation as he steadily dragged his finger over my collarbone and down between my breasts.

It continued farther. Past my belly button. Swiping

over my skin until he was at the delta of my legs, about to—

Gone. His touch disappeared and the table beneath me jostled faintly. He'd just opened a drawer. Which one was it? The *pain* one seemed unlikely, but Julius always kept me off-balance.

Strings landed gently on my chest and my brain flooded with confusion. What the . . . Oh. The flogger.

My breath caught. How was he going to use it on me? The sensation of the unknown was exciting. Was this how the women felt while on the table, at least a little bit? The curiosity was foreplay all on its own.

The flogger tails moved, sweeping downward over the curves of my bare skin. The leather caressed over my sensitive nipples, and my mouth dropped open. The sensation was nice. It made the muscles low in my belly contract with satisfaction as the tails continued their journey. It moved all the way down over my thighs and to my knees before floating away.

It sort of tickled, but was more like a wave of pleasure.

Again, the strands dropped onto my chest and began to dance over my flesh, working lower. I shuddered from their wicked stroke. It felt so freaking good. Like a skilled masseuse's hands priming my skin.

"Open your legs," Julius commanded, and I gasped. It was both strange and amazing to hear him like this. His tone was warm, yet in control, and I was more than ready to obey. I peeled my knees apart, no longer feeling shy, and when the flogger coursed over the most aroused part of me, I jerked against the restraints, stunned by the feeling.

My gasp made him chuckle. "You get it now?"

"*Yes*," I whispered. Or perhaps I pleaded. It was insane how something so simple was also so incredibly erotic.

He did it at least three more times, and each pass felt better than the last. I curled my hands around the ribbon holding my wrists to the table and arched my back, letting the leather play over every inch that was clamoring for attention.

"Fuck," he groaned appreciatively. "You've got no idea what this is doing to me."

It was almost impossible to think he was enjoying this. Sure, I was naked, but he was fully clothed and we weren't even touching. How could he be getting any pleasure from it? "This is," I said, sounding doubtful, "doing something for you?"

Sex with my ex-husband was all about the finish line for him. Was Julius merely humoring me? Pretending he was into it for my benefit?

"If you mean 'doing something for me' is getting my dick hard, then, yeah. Because it's definitely doing that."

I blinked under the blindfold. *Really?* I felt warm all over. After Tariq, I hadn't realized how desperate I was to feel desired again, and Julius made me feel that way a million times over. My bottom lip trembled and I bit down on it, holding back the urge to cry with relief. The surge of emotions was intense, and probably amplified given my current state.

"Julius," I said on a broken breath.

"I'm here."

And he was. His hot mouth locked onto mine, and I arched once more off the tabletop, straining against the straps, only this time because I wanted to throw my arms around him and kiss him until our lips were sore. His tongue tangled with mine, and the way it moved in my mouth was like he was fucking me.

I moaned, crying my need against his crushing lips, and wished I could go back in time. Back to the stupid house party where I'd run into Tariq the first weekend of my junior year and let him talk his way into my pants later that night.

I'd been so fucking stupid, lured by the glamour of dating a guy who was a football star and sure to go pro. It served me right. The bright lights on him that were so attractive at first became glaringly blinding, and I'd been trapped. I was weak. It'd been easier to stay with him and his manipulative ways, than deal with the truth. No matter what he said, Tariq was never really going to change who he was. He was never going to become a decent guy.

Julius, on the other hand, had always been one. Had what I'd wanted been right in front of me this whole time?

Something cold, metal, and kind of heavy, slipped around my wrist, just beneath the strap of ribbon. He couldn't see it beneath the blindfold, but my eyebrows pulled together. "What'd you just put on me?"

His hand skimmed over my arm, caressing. "My watch. It's gonna tell me your heartrate."

My pulse leapt. "Why do you—"

"I'm about to make you come a bunch of times. This

way I know when to back off."
>Holy.
>Shit.

Chapter FIVE

JULIUS

I had to be fucking dreaming.

Courtney was in my club. She'd kissed me. Oh yeah, and she was naked. *Naked*. My brain kept screaming it on a loop, like my eyeballs weren't working. She was so fucking gorgeous, it hurt to look at her. Her skin was like snow, her nipples were a pretty pink and her fucking body made me want to sin a thousand kind of ways.

Her fair skin looked more fucking beautiful against the black table than any girl's I'd seen. I'd stroked myself as I'd watched her writhe under the flogger. That shit was intense. I didn't play a whole lot. I sat my ass in my office chair night after night and watched other guys get their rocks off.

But, I took some notes.

I wasn't a Dominant like most of the guys who came to my club. Wasn't into pain. Or humiliation. Didn't really understand the orgasm denial shit, either. If a girl could come, why not get her there? Who was going to complain about getting too many orgasms?

I'd worn the magnetic mesh band on my watch today instead of the links, and thank fuck I had. Her wrist was tiny, but the band fit. My smartwatch said Courtney's heartrate was hovering around ninety. One-thirty or one-forty should be the peak, but the only way to know for sure was to make it happen.

I opened the second drawer and stared at my options.

The white and purple toy in the left slot was a favorite in the club. Sometimes after the client left and the girl was let out of her straps, she'd reach into the drawer and finish herself off when the guy didn't have what it took. Tara said the toy got the job done for her in less than a minute.

I pulled it from the drawer and stared at Courtney again. Fuck me. Between playing Division I ball in college and running this place, I'd seen a lot of naked women in my life. But this girl bound to the table was something else. My dick throbbed in my pants, so I grabbed it and squeezed, pushing back the feeling. I'd meant what I said, that this experience wasn't about me. It did happen to be one of my favorite things to do, though.

Making Court come her brains out? I didn't have a bigger fantasy.

She jolted when I put the round suction head of the toy against her clit and pressed the button to turn the thing on. Its buzz was quiet against her skin. The thing had to be positioned just right, so I pulled the head back and moved it up just a little higher—

"Oh my God," she groaned. Yeah, that spot was better. Her heartrate spiked upward.

One-oh-five.

One-ten. The color changed to yellow on the screen of my watch.

Her little whimpers of pleasure were the sexiest

goddamn thing ever. I put my free hand on the table and gripped the edge of the cushion. I didn't want to touch her this first time around, but keeping my hands to myself was one tall motherfucking order. Seven years I'd wanted this.

My grin went ear-to-ear. "Quit squirming or you're gonna knock it free and lose all that suction you like."

One-twenty.

Her chest was heaving and her head tipped back. Tendons in her legs flexed as she pointed her toes. Jesus, watching her was insane. My heart was going to pound right out of my ribcage.

"Oh my fucking God," she cried.

One-twenty-five. One-thirty. It climbed like a rocket, and her moans did the same, signaling an explosion. The screen blinked red, flashing the numbers as she took off.

Courtney had been a cheerleader at Ohio State, so I knew my girl could get loud, but her gasp was bigger than I'd thought it be. Damn near a scream. Louder than it'd been in my fantasies, and better sounding too. Her throaty moan that came after was a lick of heat through my spine, burning all the way to my cock.

She bucked up off the leather, straining against the straps. I tensed my grip on the table until my hand ached. *Not yet.* I wanted to touch her, but when I did, it needed to be the only feeling she had.

She shook and trembled. I could see the goddamn waves rolling down her legs and it pumped more blood straight to my dick. I was gonna bust my zipper if I got any harder.

I pulled the toy away from her skin, turned it off, and dropped it beside her on the table while she continued to come down from her O. The watch screen was yellow now as her heartrate slowed, matching her breathing. She closed her lush lips to swallow a ragged breath.

There was a drawer on the end of the table she hadn't explored. It had rubbers, lube, and other shit and I grabbed the bottle of massage oil I wanted. Jesus help me at the sight of Courtney all glistening. I could barely keep my shit together now, but was going to try it anyway.

She was still breathing hard and didn't seem to hear me uncap the bottle. I poured a bunch of the slippery liquid into my hand and rubbed my palms together to warm it up. It smelled like strawberries a little, but nothing obnoxious like a cheap stripper. It better not, either. The bottles were tiny, but fucking expensive, like they had liquid gold in them.

I leaned over the table and set my slick hands on her thighs, my thumbs on the insides of her knees. My dark hands looked so good on her creamy skin. I didn't use a lot of pressure as I glided my palms upward, working the oil over her. I ran my hands up and down, back and forth until it was distributed on her smooth thighs. Her tense muscles softened under my hands, and her head lolled to one side like she liked what I was doing.

I poured more oil into my cupped palm and smoothed it over her flat stomach. God, her body was fucking hot. As I slid the oil over her, she moved like a cat, rubbing against my touch, as if she was as fucking eager for it as I was to do it. I teased with my fingers, hinting I'd slide them down between her legs, but didn't go all the way. She needed another minute to finish recovering before I took her to the edge again.

Instead of dumping it in my hands, this time I drizzled the oil on her. I drew a thin line with it from one nipple to the other and watched the syrup-like stuff roll down the curves of her perfect tits.

She sighed when my large hands were on her, and it was the sweetest sound. I massaged and kneaded, letting her slick skin slip through my fingers. I brushed my knuckles over her hard nipples and swirled my fingertips on them. Shit, I was turned on. Sweating in my dress shirt and aching all over for her.

Her voice was breathless. "That feels so good."

"You're telling me." I squeezed her tits and loved watching the skin slide through my grip.

She moaned against the side of her arm, and the watch flashed green, telling me like a stoplight that it was time to go again. I raked my curled fingers down her body, scraping against the oiled flesh and giving her a new sensation.

"Oh," she gasped.

Her mouth dropped open and her breath cut off as I kept going, sliding two thick fingers against her pussy. She was hot and wet. I stirred her clit, and clenched my teeth to hold in a groan as she responded to my hand on her. Her glistening body contrasted against the black straps and blindfold, and was a thing of beauty. I wanted to climb on the table with her. It was built for at least two people, so it could handle me—

No, fuck it! I wasn't going to take her here like this. She had gorgeous blue eyes, and I wanted to see them when we were together. My mama didn't raise me to be a pimp, but I'd become one anyway. So, I at least wanted to have some class when it came to this. With Courtney, I wanted to do it right.

I had one hand on her tit and the other teasing her clit, and what the fuck had I done to make this shit happen? Had I just wanted it so bad and long enough to make the universe hand it to me?

The muscles of her arms strained and she moaned when I sank my middle finger inside her. She was hot as fire, and squeezed down. Her pussy clenched at my finger, so tight it got hard to see straight. Listening to her enjoy it was going to get me off if I wasn't real fucking careful.

All the rubbing I'd done on her had set the stage, and her heartrate jumped up as I thrust my finger in and out of her pretty pink pussy. "Fuck, you're sexy, Court. So fucking sexy."

Her moan walked a line between pleasure and a sob. I moved faster with both hands. The one not fucking her, glided over her shiny skin, pinching and pulling at her nipples and fumbling from one tit to the other.

Her pulse roared to one-twenty, and I recognized all the signals from last time. She was so responsive. It made me feel powerful getting her to come again so soon.

"Oh, shit!" Her moans shifted in pitch, climbing until

she gave me another gasp that could've been a scream, and her body locked up.

"Yeah, that's it," I said. "Fuck, yeah."

She bowed up from the table, and her pussy pulsed on my finger, flexing with the waves of her orgasm. My dick jerked like it needed to match her tempo. I sucked in air through my clenched teeth. It was unreal, this threat of coming in my pants when I was a grown ass man. Proof of how amazing she was.

Whatever control I had disappeared faster than a client after he'd paid.

I sank a knee on the table and hauled my big body up onto it until I was kneeling between her parted legs. Didn't give her any time to recover. I scooped my hands under her ass and lifted, lowering my head until my mouth was on her.

Maybe I startled the scream out of her, or she was still really sensitive, because my tongue on her clit made her shout my name. I closed my eyes and savored her.

Fuck my job. Fuck this club right now. I was going to make her come again, and my mouth was the best way to do it since I'd taken my cock out of the playbook. The faint strawberry taste from the oil on her skin was good. The bottle was worth every motherfucking penny.

"Holy shit," she groaned. Her legs trembled, and it got worse every time I licked her. Or maybe better. She definitely seemed to like it. And me? I fucking loved it. She was lush and soft. Her squirming made me feel like a king. I had absolute rule over her body.

When I made her come this time, her heartrate got all the way to one-forty. It probably wasn't comfortable for her in this position since her chin was stabbing her in the chest and most of her weight was on her shoulder blades.

I lowered her to the tabletop and ran my hands over her oiled skin while she flinched with aftershocks from her orgasm. I grinned at her involuntary contractions and listened to the straps go taut as she fought them.

It burst out of her in a panic. "Fuck me."

Jesus. I leaned over, put my hands on the leather on either side of her head, and slowly lowered in until I could kiss her. I stayed up on my arms though, not wanting to crush her. I mumbled it against her damp lips. "Wasn't what we agreed on."

"Let's renegotiate, then."

I laughed and slid my tongue inside her mouth, tasting her. It was probably better if she didn't say anything else. I was too close to caving. As we kissed, I tugged the blindfold up until it rested on her forehead. Her eyes fluttered open, and . . . when she looked at me? It was like she was seeing me for the first time.

Court was staring at me the way I'd always hoped she would. My chest grew six inches bigger.

"No new negotiations," I said. Could she hear the stumble in my voice? I cleared my throat, playing it off like the way she was staring in my eyes wasn't getting to me. "Once a deal's made, it's done. Club rules."

"Don't you know the owner?" she teased, but sounded half-serious.

I had to move fast. Every second the two of us were on this table, it got way more dangerous. I unlatched her wrists and the sound of Velcro tearing open filled the room. Unleashing her from the table was both good and bad. As I sat back on my heels, she climbed onto me and threw her arms around my shoulders.

It felt good holding her. Felt even better the way she was rubbing her body against my dick through my pants. We kissed like that for a long time. When her lips moved from my mouth, they trailed along my jaw and she trembled.

"I'm sorry," she whispered.

What the hell was she talking about? "Sorry for—?"

"Not coming here sooner." She babbled it out, her voice breaking and her eyes getting wet with tears. "For staying with Tariq so long, for not seeing what we—"

"Shhh," I said, trying to soothe. "Don't do that. Shit happens for a reason. I could've stopped being a pussy and come at you like I wanted to, you know." I squeezed her to me. "But if I had, we wouldn't have had this, and . . . damn. I liked how it worked out."

She smiled and blinked back her tears, clinging to me. For such a small woman, she was mighty.

And she was finally mine.

Chapter SIX

JULIUS

Courtney tried to get a hand down my pants, but I caught her wrist and stopped her. I was gonna go off too fast, and I didn't want her getting ideas I was a two-pump chump. Usually I was great at holding off, but after all we'd done on the table, and the seven years of wanting her, it made me a stick of dynamite. I needed to get my shit back together.

I told her I'd give her the rest of the tour, but it took forever to get her dressed. My fault. She was distracting as hell in a bra and underwear just as she was naked, and it was hard for her to get clothes on when my hands were always in the way.

When it was done, I trudged over to the chair and put my earpiece back in.

She ran her fingers through her hair, trying to straighten it and maybe make it so it looked like we hadn't been fucking around in the room. Not that anyone would care. Most of my employees would probably tell me it was about damn time I hooked up.

"When are you going to collect on your end of the deal?" Her eyes were bright and sexy.

"I want to tonight, but I gotta work. Tomorrow night too." The club wasn't open during the week unless I made special arrangements. "Sunday." I unrolled my sleeves and buttoned the cuffs. "You don't have an early class on Monday, right?"

She was going back to school to earn her masters in finance. On top of all the other awesome things about her, Court was book smart.

"No class on Monday at all," she said.

Good. We'd stay in bed all day, wearing each other out.

I radioed to Deiondre I was back online and to send the cleaning crew through room two.

His laugh sounded dumb through the electronics. "Audition went that good, huh?"

"Shut the fuck up, man," I snapped. "Wasn't an audition, her and me, we're—" Courtney paused. Hearing only my side of the conversation, she knew what I was about to say, and seemed real fucking interested in the label I was going to put on us. I shot her a grin, challenging her to say otherwise. "We're together."

How could she say it wasn't true? Her perfume was on my clothes and the taste of her was still in my mouth. No argument from her. Her pink, full lips turned up into that smile I loved.

We went out the door and into the hallway, and something small and soft wrapped around my hand. It was her hand, and her fingers moved until they were linked with mine. Fuck, this simple gesture was going to make me stumble. I was high off of her, like nothing could fucking stop me.

"Through that door," I pointed to the black one at the end of the hallway, "that's the payment room. It's boring in there, so we'll skip it."

I didn't take her there for a whole bunch of reasons, and one of them was I didn't want her seeing that side of this place. Joseph, the guy who'd built the club, said the magic stopped in that room. Reality set in for the clients that the fantasy was over, and it was stupid, but no way in fucking hell did I want my fantasy with Courtney to end. Ever.

We went up the narrow stairs to the second floor, her leading the way. I wanted her to go as far as she liked, rather than me in front, feeling like I was dragging her deeper into my club. I'd been in charge in the room when she was on the table, but now the roles were reversed.

"Left is my office," I said.

She dropped my hand, turned left to go in, and I watched her look around. There wasn't much to this room. A small couch faced my desk in the center, and the bank of screens the cameras fed into, was on the wall behind it. My office was windowless. Joseph had tried to make it look classy to match the rest of the place, but it didn't feel sexy.

It felt like business.

"This is where I run things. When we get busy," I said, being a shitty tour guide, "someone else helps watch the feeds."

She turned to face me and licked her lips. She was nervous?

"What?" I asked.

"Can I, uh . . . *help*?"

"Stay and watch?" Jesus, she wanted to sit beside me

while this place was operating? I pictured it. It turned me on all over again, and I'd just gotten my dick to cooperate. "You wanna?"

Her shoulders lifted. "I'm . . . interested in seeing it."

"Never done that before," I said. "But I can swing it. I know the owner."

Her small laugh sounded so good. She walked to the desk, trailed her fingers over the wood, and turned away to look at the bank of screens. In room two, a woman rolled a cleaning cart up to the table.

Court's shoulders tightened and her voice was hesitant. "Why didn't you tell me about this place? Are you . . . embarrassed?"

Oh, fuck. I swallowed hard. "Nah, it's not that."

"Because I'm not going to judge you, Julius."

She'd given me back my watch, and if I'd still had the app running, the screen would be red. My pulse kicked hard. "I know you wouldn't."

She turned to face me. Even confused, she was still so fucking beautiful. Her blue eyes peered up. "Then, why'd you keep it from me?"

If we had a chance at long-term, I needed to come clean with her about everything. I sucked in a deep breath and prayed I wasn't going to fuck this all up. I wanted to do the right thing. Better late than never, right? "I don't want secrets between us no more."

I put one foot in front of the other and made my way to her. She didn't move as I lifted my hand and set it on her cheek, but her pupils got big and she tensed. She sensed whatever I was about to say was gonna be serious.

I got it out quick, like it'd be less painful that way, which was stupid. It was going to hurt her no matter what. "Tariq came here."

She jolted. "When? After the divorce?"

I opened my dumb mouth, but nothing came out, and her eyes turned hard. She stepped backward, out of my hold.

Her tone was razor-sharp. "When?"

She thought it was just one time, because that was probably all her self-preservation would let her. Spared her the worst of it. Tariq had cheated and lied to her for years, and he'd forced me to do it too, but no more. I was fucking done.

"Courtney." I wanted to soften the blow, but couldn't. "He was a regular."

She gasped like I'd tackled her, and she threw her arms over her chest. It was defensive. Trying to protect herself from the terrible shit I'd hidden.

I'd never felt so miserable in my goddamn life. It hurt like a motherfucker watching her suffer. "I'm so fucking sorry. I didn't run this place when he first came around—"

"A regular," she spat at me. Fire was in her eyes, and they burned hotter as she put it all together. "Wait a goddamn minute. He was coming here before you took over?" Her face twisted with horror. "Tariq was fucking girls at this club for years . . . *and you knew about it?*"

My mouth was bone dry. My throat closed up, but I pushed the word out anyway. It was quiet and guilty as hell. "Yeah." My arms weighed a million pounds, dragging my shoulders down. "I wanted to tell you, I fucking swear, but Tariq . . . He was on the list before I found out."

Joseph had a strict policy about clients' identities staying secret—and me? I followed rules. So many years of football made it impossible not to. I put order and loyalty on top of everything else. I did what the boss said, right up until I got to be the boss.

It wasn't an excuse, and she wasn't having it, either. Courtney's face was still stuck on horror. "How the fuck could you not tell me?"

"He made me promise and he was supposed to be my boy." It sounded even worse saying it out loud. "It fucking killed me, knowing. I told him every goddamn time how he was fucking everything up, but he wouldn't listen. Jesus, I'm so sorry."

Her face crumbled, and panic gripped me. I was supposed to be her friend and I'd betrayed her. And, shit, I was gonna lose her over this.

"Keeping my mouth shut about Tariq was the biggest mistake I ever made," I said.

She pulled her shoulders back, trying to look strong. "You're right. And getting on the table downstairs was mine."

It would have stung less if she'd slapped me. I stood motherfucking paralyzed as she pushed past me and stormed toward the door. She was almost through it when I snapped back into action. "Wait. Please, Court."

She didn't.

I chased after her, my big footsteps booming on the

stairs as we went down. She was moving so fast, it was almost a sprint, and then it was. She hit the door to the front lounge and barreled through it.

I pushed the button on my comm pack. "D, where you at?"

He didn't get a chance to answer because Courtney pushed open the door to the security entrance and ran face-first into his chest. She bounced off of him and rolled right, moving toward the door to the street.

Deiondre got one look at my face and went for the door, beating her to it. He threw his black ass in front of it, stopping her, but like I'd taught him, he kept his tone friendly, no matter the situation. "Hold up a sec, girl."

"Get the fuck outta my way."

Deiondre was like twice her size, but even he flinched at her cold words. It sliced at me. Courtney was my best friend. I'd made her laugh, seen her cry, but I'd never heard her sound like *him* before. Five years being married to Tariq, and this was the first time she'd done it.

"C'mon, let's talk about this," I pleaded.

She barely moved her head, like I wasn't worth the trouble. She turned just enough to give me a profile. "No. I can't even look at you right now."

She shut down and shut me out. There was no getting through to her right now. Time was what she needed. I looked at my security guard and nodded for him to step back. "It's cool, D."

As soon as he was out of the way, she shoved the door open and fled.

He lifted an eyebrow at me. "She's pissed."

Yeah, no shit. "Can you walk with her to the train station? Make sure no one bothers her." My club wasn't exactly in a nice part of town.

"You got it."

He disappeared out the door, leaving me alone in the boring-looking entryway, and I put my hands on my hips. I was more fucked up now than I'd been when I got here, worried about Courtney going out with someone else.

I hated the lying. I hated how I'd hurt her.

But I was going to make it right. I just needed a motherfucking plan.

Chapter SEVEN

COURTNEY

I didn't answer Julius's texts or calls during the weekend. Whenever I thought about him, I see-sawed between anger and hurt. I got that Tariq had been Julius's friend first, but how could he not tell me something so . . . *huge*?

Julius's silence was deafening.

Six months ago, Tariq got drunk after an away game and he'd thought he was texting his driver to pick him up from some random chick's place. Instead, he'd been texting me. I remember the moment with horrifying clarity as I looked at my phone and read it. My husband bragged about the nasty pussy he'd gotten in two texts that were so full of spelling errors, some words were gibberish.

Autocorrect gave up on him, and that night, I finally did too.

He'd cheated on me when we were dating, but I'd foolishly believed he'd change, and forgave him. But Tariq was always going to be who he was, and he didn't apologize for it, either. He'd come home from the trip and before I let him say a word, I announced we were getting a divorce.

His gaze left mine and dropped down to his expensive Italian shoes. "I can't be with just one girl, Nene," he said, using his nickname for me that I tolerated, but never really liked. "I tried, but I ain't built that way."

It was a bullshit excuse, and I told him so as he left.

We never had kids, thank God. He wanted them, and I did too, but things got rocky a while back after he'd torn his ACL and couldn't play the rest of the season. A baby would only make the strain on our marriage worse. If I got pregnant, I'd never leave him, and deep down I knew I needed to. We weren't meant for each other.

I was a fool, but not stupid.

I knew the night of the drunken texts wasn't the first time Tariq had been unfaithful, but hearing he'd been a club regular for years . . . I felt shattered all over again. Who else knew? Were the other players and their wives laughing at clueless Courtney, who was too dumb to know her husband couldn't keep his dick in his pants? That he'd willingly pay to fuck other women, rather than sleep with his own wife?

What did Julius think of me?

He'd been so angry on my behalf when I'd broken down and showed him the texts. He'd been the one to suggest Kyle McCreary as an attorney when I told him I'd asked Tariq for a divorce. He'd said I deserved so much better than Tariq.

Julius was right about that.

I deserved a guy who I could trust, and those were apparently in short supply these days.

Sunday afternoon was spent in the gym, where I could send his calls rolling in to voicemail while I tried to climb away my feelings on the stair machine. I knew I couldn't avoid him forever. He was my friend, and I wasn't going to throw our entire friendship away over what he'd kept from me, but I wasn't happy, and I needed to get the point across.

My legs were rubber as I got home and dragged myself into the shower. Afterward, I cinched my hair up in a towel, pulled on a pair of old cheerleading sweats, and started thinking about options for dinner. I didn't have the desire to order out, but was feeling too lazy to make something—

A knock on my front door made me nearly jump out of my skin.

I treaded slowly to the door and raised up on my toes to look through the peep hole, but I already suspected who it was. I sighed loudly as I opened the door and glared up at him, only to have the air cut off in my lungs.

Julius's suit was midnight blue. He had a simple white dress shirt beneath the coat and a gold-striped tie. I still wasn't used to seeing him in suits, and this one . . . he looked amazing in it. Every bit the man who'd given me the best orgasms of my life, and hadn't asked for anything in return.

Well, that probably wasn't true. He was likely here to ask my forgiveness.

"I'm not ready to talk about it," I said flatly.

"You don't got to. We can talk about whatever you want."

He stepped into my apartment without an invitation, and I pushed the door closed behind him with too much force. It shut with a loud bang.

He gave me a once-over. I had on old sweats and no makeup, but of course he looked at me like it didn't matter at all. His gaze settled on the towel wrapped around my hair. "Better get a move on," he said. "Our reservation's at six-thirty."

My jaw dropped to my knees. "What?"

His dark eyes sharpened, studying me. "It's Sunday. We got a date."

I took a step back. I didn't like being so close to him or smelling his cologne, but I couldn't outrun the reminder of Friday night. I could still feel the cold leather of the table against my heated skin. I still felt the lingering pleasure he'd given me, and he hadn't even needed to take his clothes off to deliver it. What would it be like if he had?

Wait, no. I didn't want to think about that. I scowled. "Are you shitting me?"

"We made a deal."

"No. It's off." He'd lied for more than a year.

One step was all it took, and he was right in front of me, so close my breasts would brush his chest if I took a deep breath. His eyes were soft and warm. "I know you're mad. You got every right."

I was defenseless against him when he was wearing armor made of fine blue wool and gold silk. I stood like a statue as he hesitantly moved in, setting one hand on my waist. The warmth of it seeped beneath the cotton of my shirt.

"But," he said on a low voice, "I held up my end of the deal, and now you're gonna hold up yours, Court."

My voice faltered. "What are you gonna do? Make me?"

He was prepared for that. "I can be persuasive." A light smile tugged across his lips. "If that fails, I got other ways."

"Other ways?" I repeated.

"We have a verbal agreement and I'm betting my attorney agrees."

It was clear Julius was kidding, but my eyes went down to slits. "Keep Kyle out of this—" Except I was a hypocrite now, wasn't I? I'd gotten Kyle involved with my fake date scheme, trying to force Julius into action.

His other hand rested gently on my waist, and I allowed him to hold me. I told myself it was because I was too tired from my workout to move, and not because I liked the feeling of his hands on my body.

"No," I said. "I'm not going." On the ridiculous date, or leaving his hold?

Julius's expression sobered. "You don't want to, I'll give you an 'out.' You let me say my part about Tariq, and when I'm done, I'll go."

"I told you, I'm not ready to talk about it."

He looked almost pleased with my answer. "Okay. So, put on that red dress and let's go."

My face heated with annoyance. It'd probably match the dress perfectly. "I said no—" He picked me up like I was nothing, squeezing a gasp from me as he put me over his shoulder. "What the hell?"

I bounced against him as he marched toward my bedroom, and could feel the vibrations of his deep voice through his back. "I said I'd tried to persuade you."

"Put me down!"

We made it through the doorway and he did as I asked, dropping me gently onto the edge of my unmade bed. I glared up at him.

"I didn't make my move when I should have, but no more. You're gonna let me talk about this, or put on the dress." His eyes were desperate. "Pick one."

"Fine," I said in a huff. "I agreed to dinner, so I'll go, but don't expect me to say anything."

"You're gonna go the whole night without a word?" He couldn't have looked more skeptical if he'd tried.

So, I could be a bit of a talker, but if needed I could be—oh, shit. *The whole night.* I'd forgotten the final term of our deal. Date. Red dress. Night in his bed. There was no way I'd stay mute through all that, but his dubious expression made me desperate to try.

He'd stayed quiet for more than a year. Couldn't I be silent for one night?

I gave him a hard, determined look before launching to my feet. I pulled the towel off my head, shoved it in his chest, and pushed him toward the door. "I'm changing, so get out."

Chapter
EIGHT

COURTNEY

Candles flickered on the tabletop and added to the subdued lighting of the Italian restaurant Julius brought me to. It was a white tablecloth kind of place, with a fancy wine list as long as a novel, and tables tucked into quiet alcoves to make it feel intimate.

Our little table for two was romantic as fuck, and if he'd brought me here last week, I'd have climbed over it to get on him. But everything was different now. His withheld secret was a wall too tall for me to get over without his help.

So far, so good. I didn't talk during the ride here. I'd sat in the passenger seat of his Range Rover wearing the red dress, and tried not to think about what we'd done on Friday night.

He'd told me the truth, when he could have continued to keep me in the dark. It was doubtful I'd have figured it out on my own. Why had he told me? It would have been so much easier for him if he hadn't.

The only time I spoke was to order my drink and then dinner. Julius bypassed the wine list. The front for his illegal business was a wine club. It had been the first thing to make me question his story because Julius didn't even like the stuff.

When I didn't talk, he didn't either, but he acted as if it was no big deal. He was comfortable with the lack of conversation, but it drove me insane. I made it until the salads were delivered, and then . . . I pathetically broke.

"You knew my husband was cheating on me," I blurted out.

Julius stopped mid-sip of his cocktail. He lowered the glass slowly and looked at the ice cubes floating inside, resigned. "It's worse than that."

Oh my God. My hands curled on the armrests and I dug my fingernails in. "How the hell is it worse?"

If I wasn't already so hurt, I would have been overwhelmed with sadness at his expression. He looked crushed. "I took his money."

I closed my eyes, which were burning with tears. Maybe I'd been wrong. Maybe this was too much to overcome. Too much damage for our friendship to survive.

"I'm a proud man, but I'm not too proud to tell you it made me sick. Fucking sick to my stomach about what he was doing, and that I let the asshole get away with it." He plunked his drink down on the table and the ice sloshed in the glass. "It's a shitty excuse, but my club went through some scary shit last year. Legal stuff. I was worried if I cut Tariq off, he'd fuck everything up."

Julius leaned forward across the table and his gaze was focused. "Now, me? I don't care about me. I can handle my problems. But the folks who work for me, they're good people. I didn't want none of them dragged down if the club fell."

That sounded like typical Julius. He'd fall on his sword before he let anyone else die by it. I stared at the empty appetizer plate before me on the table, unable to look my friend in the eye.

"You should have told me," I choked out. "You're my best friend, right? I thought you were in my corner. I mean, you helped me through this whole thing . . . but you didn't say a goddamn word." My throat grew scratchy as the emotions welled up. "I can't handle any more lies, Julius. I won't deal with another guy who breaks my trust."

"I know. You deserve a hell of a lot better. I made a huge mistake, but you can trust me, I swear."

I didn't know what else to say. "You should have fucking told me."

"Yeah. I'm so sorry." His sincere tone drew my gaze up like it was magnetic. "I'll make it right if you'll let me. Please tell me you can get past this. Maybe not tonight, but eventually. I gotta know. If this is the end, I wanna get it over with."

I swallowed a breath. *The end?* I was angry and hurt, but he knew he'd fucked up. He was trying to apologize, and I believed in second chances. Didn't I?

You gave Tariq one, and look how well it turned out. It wasn't fair to compare them, thought. Julius was nothing like my ex-husband. I knew in my heart Julius was a good man, and I couldn't stand the idea of losing him.

"It's . . . not the end."

Relief poured through his handsome face, and I fought back the next swell of emotions. I wanted to forgive him. It was in my nature to be forgiving, as long as there was regret. It was something Tariq had never shown me. Guilt? Sure. But he didn't apologize. His only regret was at getting caught. Losing me felt like failure, and my ultra-competitive ex-husband didn't like that.

"Is that it?" I asked. "You didn't tell me the truth because you thought Tariq was going to fuck everything—"

"No." Julius cut me off, but his eyes shifted away. He was nervous about something.

"Tell me the truth," I demanded. "No more secrets."

His gaze settled back on mine, and he looked like a man who was heading for his doom. "I didn't say nothing because I thought you'd forgive him again and I'd lose you." He made a face. "Not like you were mine, but I couldn't stand you being with him while you knew he was running around with girls on the side."

"I wouldn't," I said, but it came out weak. I had taken Tariq back before. Julius was right to be concerned I'd do it again.

"I was scared, okay? I didn't want to hurt you. I should have thrown his ass out a long time ago. I'm fucking sorry I didn't sooner."

I straightened my posture in surprise. "You threw him out?" Julius's friendship with Tariq had fallen apart, but I assumed it was the divorce and how Julius had sided with me. "Is this the reason you don't talk to him anymore?"

He blinked slowly. "I don't talk to him because of the way he treated you. He's a selfish piece of shit, and he ain't worth my time. If I wasn't in love with you, I'd have stopped being friends with him a long time ago."

My heart lurched to a halt. The sound in the restaurant dropped out altogether. "What?"

It rolled out of his mouth casually, but dropped on the table like a bomb. "I think you heard me."

Love . . .? Words were a jumbled mess in my head. I couldn't sort them out into sentences that made any sense, so I uttered the only thing I could remember how to say. "What?"

"No more secrets." He wasn't fazed by my repeated response. His expression was intense and too powerful to be anything other than pure truth. "I love you. I have for a while now."

Finally, my mouth and brain could get it together. "How long?"

"About seven years."

"Oh my God." *Oh my God!*

"You know when I knew? We were at some party. You were standing in a crowded kitchen by the keg. T had gone to the bathroom or something, and left you with me. You remember it?" He didn't give me time to process his question fully. Was he talking about the night we met? Julius's eyes drifted upward for a moment as he recalled the memory. "This guy comes in, wearing a dinosaur costume. Wasn't Halloween. No clue why he was wearing it."

"Him and his friends always dressed up for the games," I babbled, reeling from the revelation. "That way they'd get on the Jumbotron."

"Oh, yeah." Julius smiled. "People are giving him

shit about it. Someone asks what he's supposed to be, and he says he's a lesbian. It was weird between you and me, cause we'd just met and T was MIA, so I was trying to make conversation, and asked if you thought the dinosaur guy looked like a lesbian. You said, yeah. That he looked like a—"

"Oh my God." I blurted it out now, just as I'd done then. "Lick-a-lotta-puss. I was so drunk."

His grin widened. "You went as red as the bow in your hair. It was so fucking cute, Court. I didn't stand a chance." The playful look faded back into his serious one. "But you were already with him, and I wasn't gonna get in the way. I wanted you to be happy."

It was a gut-punch right in my feels. What he wanted didn't matter. He always put others first. The irony of it all was a hard lump to swallow. Being with Tariq hadn't made me happy, but I suspected the opposite could be true of the man sitting across from me.

Julius was in love with me. Could I feel the same about him some day?

"Why did you tell me?" I asked. "I mean, about Tariq being a regular? I never would have found out if you hadn't."

"I want everything in the clear. Don't want him to have anything to do with us." His gaze clouded. "I know my club's got a taste that isn't for everyone, and what I do ain't respectable. Still, the only time I ever felt dirty, was when he was there."

His pained expression made me believe it, and what he was saying . . . he'd broken the trust between us to try to build it stronger.

"I'm sorry," he started.

I shook my head. "No, I am. I'm sorry for what I said at the club, that getting on the table was a mistake. I was lashing out—"

His shoulders relaxed with a sigh of relief. "You don't got to apologize."

"I do, because it was a lie and I don't want to lie to you. Nothing we did felt like a mistake."

Emotions swirled inside me, twisting me up and making it hard to find the courage to put myself out there. My heart was fragile now. Not quite done with rehab, although the beautiful man across the table was doing all he could to help. He'd do anything for me, including telling me a difficult truth. And he'd been brave enough to say he loved me, not knowing if I'd ever return that love.

I remembered how it felt when we'd connected for the first time in a kiss. Not a mistake at all. I stared at him and filled my expression with longing. "Being with you felt . . . right."

He'd been fast on the football field, but he moved so quickly, it hadn't registered he'd left his seat until his mouth was on mine. His hands tangled in my hair as he bent over my chair, kissing me and not giving a fuck who was watching.

It put our previous passion to shame. I gripped the lapels of his jacket, tugging him closer as his lips slayed me.

"Jesus," I whispered, echoing his word after our first kiss.

He chuckled and dropped another kiss on my lips, although this one was tame. Restrained. He lingered for a long moment, giving me a silent promise of more . . . but later.

"Seven years catching up with me," he joked.

"With us," I corrected, giving him the brightest smile I had.

Chapter NINE

COURTNEY

We ate dinner like a pair of starving wolves, although I don't think either of us was actually hungry for food. The faster we finished, the faster we could be alone and on to the final term of our deal. Would we go straight to his bedroom when we got to his place?

Nope. Neither of us could wait that long after the car ride to his apartment. It'd been so heavy with sexual tension, I felt like an overly wound spring. One touch and I'd explode.

I'd been to his place a few times before, but we mostly hung out at mine. He was a guy's guy, and didn't do much with the apartment. Only, things were way different than the last time I'd been here. I barely got a look before he descended on me.

"You have curtains," I said with surprise as he pressed me against a wall and buried his face in the side of my neck.

His mouth latched onto the sensitive skin below my ear and sucked, and it sent pleasure coursing through me. I closed my eyes and sank an inch down the wall. Holy shit, that felt good.

I was too low for him. He slid his hands down the backs of my legs, and in one quick jerk, he had me lifted and pinned to the wall, supporting me with his hands on my ass. The short skirt of the dress corded around my waist. This change in position was so much better. It made it easier to kiss him. Easier to squeeze my thighs around his hips and rock against him, grinding our lower bodies together.

There were paintings hung on the wall, replacing the old OSU poster he'd taped up. A golden pattern filled the oversize canvases and gave the room a sunny feeling. They were big, and warm. Just like him.

Julius's bulk, even from the moment I'd met him, never intimidated me. He didn't act aggressive unless provoked, and in his dominating presence, all I felt was safe. The feeling intensified as I was held against the wall, cradled in his arms so he could shower kisses along the slope of my neck.

I shivered as his breath rolled down the low-cut neckline of my dress, and I arched my back, thrusting my breasts in his face. He murmured a quiet approval, and just the sound of it was delicious.

I'd spent years mastering balance and core strength for cheerleading. I was no stranger to being lifted by a strong guy. I was comfortable being launched high in the air and tumbling without disorientation. Yet, all that practice didn't prepare me for this. Three feet off the ground and held steady in Julius's thick arms made me off-balance and dizzy.

I was going to fall, but only metaphorically.

I cupped my hands on his cheeks and kissed him with total abandon. Like it was the most natural thing. But the world was spinning and I gripped him tighter—

It wasn't the earth that was suddenly moving, it was him. He pulled us away from the wall and carried me toward his couch. He turned at the last moment, dropping down to sit so I was in his lap, straddling him.

"Is this couch new?" I asked.

He was distracted as his hands slid up my back, searching for the zipper. "Yeah. I got a decorator. She finished last week."

A decorator? I smiled. He wasn't a boy anymore, and he had a grown-up apartment to prove it. I craned my neck and took a good look at the place. It was sophisticated and manly, but still . . . friendly. Easy and inviting.

Everything reminded me exactly of him.

"She's good," I murmured as he inched my zipper down. "Do you have her card?"

"Nah, Noemi's a friend. Does the decorating shit as a hobby." His hands slowed as he tugged at the strap of my dress, easing it over my shoulder. His voice went low. "You really wanna talk about my couch and curtains right now?"

He leaned forward, pressing his damp lips to my newly-exposed skin.

"No," I said breathlessly. Goosebumps burst from his soft kiss, radiating outward, and my heart skipped faster as his mouth worked lower. He peeled the dress and my bra down, inch by painfully slow inch, kissing my skin until I was shaking with anticipation.

Hell no, I didn't want to talk about decorating. My mind emptied of any thought except the way his soft lips felt traveling over my breasts, moving determinedly toward my nipples. They'd tightened into aching knots and I was eager for satisfaction.

"Oh," I sighed as I got my wish.

He sucked and nipped at me. The pull on my sensitive skin sent a rush of heat to my center. I yanked my arms out of the dress and bra straps, letting the fabric fall to my waist. His mouth was erotic, and worked in perfect combination with his hands, gripping me just as firm as I wanted him to.

I squirmed in his lap, both getting relief and yet needing more. The months without a partner had amped up my sex drive until I barely recognized myself. I reached behind and set a hand on his knee for support so I could lean back and arch even more, presenting my body to him like he was a king and I was his to claim.

Large, slightly calloused hands splayed over my topless form, and Julius made a sound of deep satisfaction. His gaze on me was heavy, full of lust. It was searing.

His tie was smooth and soft as I curled a fist around it and yanked him to me, demanding his mouth's attention on me once again, and he was happy to obey. It sent me into a frenzy. I wanted to go down on him, but I wanted his fingers inside me. And I needed his tongue between my legs, working me over until I was a shaking mess. And, God, I *needed* to fuck him, and him to fuck me, and . . . and . . .

This thing between us started as a tiny spark but had exploded into a fire so magnificent, it threatened to consume me. I backed off the couch, climbing out of his lap, and he moved with the same urgency I did.

Only, he was trying to pull my dress down, and even unzipped, the waist of it would never fit over my hips. Our hands tangled, trying to pull it in opposite directions when we had the same goal. We both wanted it gone.

His handsome face was etched with concentration and a laugh broke from me. "Up," I said. "That's how it has to come off."

He grinned. As he pulled up, I slid down, getting on my knees between his parted legs and leaving him holding the dress. As he tossed it to the side, he looked at me with surprise, but I flashed him the sultriest smile I possessed.

"You're not going to help me?" I teased as I undid his belt buckle. He slumped down to make it easier for me to get his pants undone, but his hands threaded lightly through my hair.

His voice was uneven. "I can't. I've been wanting it so long— *Fuck*."

When I dropped his zipper, my fingers brushed over the hard bulge packed inside his pants, and he shuddered with pleasure. He lifted his hips when I tugged on the waistband of his underwear, and it was just enough to get the elastic down, unleashing him.

"Oh, Jesus." I came to a screeching halt.

There was a stereotype for black men, and it was one my ex-husband didn't fill. But Julius? Oh, yes, he did. I lifted my concerned gaze to meet his, and his eyes had a hint of pride.

One of his hands slipped down to cup my cheek and

he brushed his thumb over my lips. "Don't worry." He sounded sweet and perhaps amused. "I bet we figure it out."

Despite my surprise, I smiled.

His fingers moved as he worked to undo the knot at the top of his tie. His dark-eyed gaze pinned me to the floor while he slowly slid the tie free from his neck and dropped the gold silk on top of my discarded red dress.

His eyes hooded when I wrapped my fingers around him, squeezing at the base. Gentle at first as I stroked upward, and then harder as I pushed my fist down. He groaned so deep, it sounded like it verged on pain. But his face said it was one hundred percent pleasure.

His skin was soft as velvet, but he was hard as could be in my hands. I pumped on him, watching the motion with excited curiosity. The picture of my grip twisting down his length was so sexy, I was going to burn up inside. I loved seeing him coil and flex in reaction to my touch, and listening to his short breath, punctuated by groans.

I shifted on my knees, settling into a more comfortable position, and leaned forward, bringing my lips to the dark tip of his cock. He jerked and swore in response, but his hand went rigid in my hair, urging me to stay.

Urging me to do it.

I swiped my tongue over the sensitive underside, and followed the ridge around the head. One circuit, and then I opened my mouth, and made my best attempt to take him inside.

"Mother. Fucking. Shit." His head flopped down onto the back of the couch with a loud thud. "I wanna watch but . . . damn, girl. Feels so good."

It was the shortest blowjob in the history of blowjobs, and for the first time in my life, I was disappointed it was over. Julius jammed his hands under my arms and hauled me up, only to push me down onto my back on the seat of the couch. My short blonde hair splashed in my face, and as I swiped it out of my eyes, I stared up at the enormous man kneeling over me on the couch.

He undid the line of buttons on his shirt so fast, it was stunning, and when he pulled the dress shirt off, I held my breath. He was . . . exquisite. All curves and muscles stretched over a quiet warrior's frame. I reached up. I set my small hand against his wide, hardened chest and felt the strong heartbeat thump beneath it.

His hand covered mine, holding it pressed to his heart for a long moment, and I had to break his gaze and look away before the emotions got to me. We teetered between lust and passion, trying to find a balance between.

He held onto my hand as he lowered down and set his lips on mine, and when his tongue dipped into my mouth, we tottered back toward lust. His kiss was greedy and . . . *sexy*. Oh, God, it was amazing how sexy he could make me feel when his tongue caressed mine, sliding in my mouth and coaxing a moan out of me.

It was why he caught me off guard. He eased a hand between my back and the cushion, and lifted, sliding me across the couch until my shoulder blades were on the armrest. He was making more room for himself at the other end. I swallowed a deep breath and closed my eyes so I could enjoy the sensation better, mimicking the blindfold. He licked a line down my body, leaving a damp trail that was cool in the air swirling around us.

My belly quivered as the tip of his tongue coasted over it, heading further south. His shoulders eased between my thighs, and he put his hands beneath my legs, cradling them.

The room was quiet, other than my ragged breathing and the soft, sexy kisses he placed on me. He didn't focus on one spot, either. He kissed the insides of my thighs, low on my stomach, the hollow where my leg met my body. I flinched at the contact of his lips right at the edge of my panties.

Julius lifted his head and stared up at me from between my legs, and even his breath's featherlight touch was feeding into my desire. He didn't have to use words. I knew what he wanted. I lifted my hips and let him peel the black lace from my body, and he kissed my legs as he did it.

I felt worshiped.

It was like going down on me was a bigger treat for him than it was for me, and the idea almost made me giggle. Did this man have any idea how good he was with his mouth? Because he was insane. Women would kill each other to get to him if they knew.

"Shit, yes," I moaned as his tongue glanced over my clit.

One long lick and my knees shook. He made a noise of contentment, and I nearly lost it right then. Hearing how much he liked it was erotic. He cradled my hips, tilting me to a better angle, and I ran my hands over his arms.

He teased me. His indecent kiss wouldn't stay on my clit for long. He planted more kisses on me, just to the side of where I wanted them, all while his hands slid over my body. I bowed my back as he squeezed my breast and pinched a nipple.

"Mmm," I moaned when his mouth returned to the spot I needed it to be.

And again, my response was echoed by him. It was a chain reaction. When I grew louder, so did he, and it escalated until we were both sighing and moaning together. I hung over the armrest with my head tipped back, gasping for air as heat drilled into me. His tongue was urgent, fluttering and slashing, causing me to writhe on the cushions.

My knees were up and my feet hanging in the air, and whenever I moved too much, Julius would steady me with a hand on the underside of my thigh. He held me open so he could keep giving me pleasure like I'd never had before. I clawed at the cording on the edge of the couch cushions, and stroked my hands along his shoulders. I was wild and desperate.

The need swelled and swelled until I couldn't hold back anymore. It burst from me in a torrent of pleasure, ripping through my system and firing along every nerve ending.

"Yes, yes . . . *yes*," I cried.

He gasped loudly, like the amazing sensation washing through me was roaring right through him. I bucked, jerking away from his tongue, too sensitive to take another touch, and he pulled back, watching me as I came apart.

Half undressed, pants undone and sagging around his thighs, he looked powerful and gorgeous. The way he looked at me with his expressive eyes made his words from earlier echo in my head.

How could I not fall for this man? I didn't stand a chance.

Chapter TEN

JULIUS

Courtney's chest was heaving. She had her eyes closed and a hand on her forehead, looking like I'd put her through the wringer. But then she gave me a blissed-out smile, and I felt twenty goddamn feet tall.

The noises she'd made when I was going down on her . . . *Jesus*. If I was a weaker man, they'd have killed me. Those soft moans. The gasps. Her whimpers. My cock jerked again even as the sound faded from my ears.

Her eyes fluttered open in time to see me slide my first two fingers in my mouth. She was already wet, and I'd gotten her to come, but a little more prep wasn't gonna hurt anything.

Her lips rounded into a silent 'oh' as I worked my first finger inside her. She was draped over the edge of the couch, her tits pointing to the ceiling, and looking at them made my mouth water. Wait a minute. Every fucking inch of her did that.

I was up on my knees and gripped the back of the couch to keep my shit stable. She was tight, and I didn't want to hurt her, but I'd barely gotten the second finger in when she—

"Please," she said. "I want you."

Aw, fuck. I scooped my hands under her back and

lifted, moving us so I was sitting again and she was on me like she was when I first moved us to the couch. Except, she was naked and my dick was out, and I needed my motherfucking wallet more than air.

I sucked on her tits as I fumbled in my pockets and finally jerked the fold of leather free. I flipped it open, pulled out the condom, and dropped the rest of it to the ground. I had what I needed now.

Her hands were on my head, holding me while I tried to do two things at once. Her tits were distracting as hell. It took longer than it should have to tear the packet open, but when she heard it, she sat back and watched me put it on.

I'd wanted our first time to be in a bed, but the couch was good. Better. She'd be on top and set the pace. Which she'd need to do, since the size of my dick seemed to be a surprise.

Her tiny waist felt so good in my hands, I let them hang out there. She said she wanted me, and I gave her a look that said, "*C'mon and get it.*"

She laced her fingers together behind my neck, and her eyes got big as hell as she rose on her knees, shifting over me. I waited to see her lick her lips and show me she was nervous, but it didn't happen. Her blue eyes stared back at me, and my chest tightened. Seven long years I'd hoped something like this would happen.

I reached between us and grabbed myself at the base, holding still so she could lower down. But she lingered, hovering.

"Oh, Jesus, Court. You gotta—"

Her hands gripped the back of my neck and her pupils grew so big, her eyes were black. Our mouths fell open at the same time, and we exhaled loudly as I pushed inside. Her throat bobbed as she swallowed, and her arms shook with tension.

"Fuck, am I hurting you?" I asked, trying to stay calm.

She blinked and gave a weird smile, like I'd just asked a dumb fucking question. "God, no." Her warm forehead pressed against mine. "I'm just trying to remember this."

I kissed her. Deep and slow, showing her I could fuck the same way if that was what she wanted. We had all night. We had tomorrow too. Maybe a lifetime, if I was a lucky enough motherfucker.

But she moved on me, using her body to say *slow* wasn't gonna do it for her. She worked her hips and I nudged further inside, all the way until I fit. Her pussy was tight as a fist. Hot, and wet, and I nearly died and went to heaven when she began to fuck me.

"Oh," she whispered. "Oh, I like this."

She was gonna kill me. Cause of death: Courtney Crawford. It was a great way to go.

"Yeah?" I said softly against her ear. "How about this?"

I squeezed her hips, getting her to stay in place, and then I moved beneath her. I thrust into her hot body, which felt so good I was gonna go out of my damn mind. I should've gone slower. Maybe not as deep. But she moaned and dropped her head onto my shoulder, and rode me like she loved it.

I put my hands on her ass, pushing and pulling her to ride me faster. That got her whimpers started. She bit down on my shoulder and it made me drive harder. Finally, my mouth slammed against hers, and she kept up with me, not breaking the kiss.

We got sweaty. Out of breath. She was trembling and twitching, and it was un-fucking-likely I was gonna last much longer. Not with the way her tits were bouncing from my hard thrusts, or her moans that were so sexy, they should have come with an explicit content label.

I pushed her hair out of our way as we kissed, and skimmed my fingers down her body. Lots of girls didn't come from regular sex, and Court was one of them. I knew because she'd gotten plastered after we went out and celebrated her signing the divorce papers, and her drunk lips told me all sorts of intimate shit I prayed wouldn't get me friend-zoned for life.

I'd had to jerk off when I got home, thinking about how I'd try to make it happen for her.

I pressed the pads of my fingers to her clit and stirred as she hammered down on my cock. This shit was getting intense, and dire. I wanted to come. It boiled in my veins. But I really wanted her to get there first.

"Oh, shit," she gasped. She rocked against my hand, finding a rhythm she liked.

"That's it," I said. Everything was picking up. Her tempo. My heartrate. Her moans. My urge to go off.

"Julius, right there. Oh, fuck, right there. *Right there . . .*" she trailed off. As her words got softer, her tremors got bigger. I stirred my fingers, rubbing furiously, and the cry she let out was the sweetest fucking reward. Her muscles locked up and her pussy clamped down, strangling my dick.

Sent me right over the edge with her.

I came in a rush of fire. It burned hot, and then freezing cold with each burst, and the pleasure was fucking unbelievable. My heartbeat got all fucked up, speeding along. I groaned my satisfaction, letting it roll from deep in my chest.

She was still shaking when it was over. Her body pulsed an aftershock and I jerked inside her. The feeling was overwhelming. There was nothing else I could do but sit there and kiss the shit out of her. It was all I wanted to do anyway.

Eventually, she slowly pulled off and collapsed beside me on the couch. I was burning up, but also disappointed she wasn't on me anymore.

"You okay?" I asked. I tried not to hold my breath.

"I'm great." She gave me playful side-eye. "And also, I'm not made of glass."

"Didn't say you were." I pretended I wasn't relieved and acted casual. "You thirsty?"

She nodded.

I got up and went into the kitchen. First order of business was to ditch the condom. I washed my hands, then grabbed two cans of Bud Light from the fridge. "Don't be putting any clothes back on," I said loudly. Her body was too amazing. I might spend the rest of the night just looking at her.

Who the fuck was I kidding? I had lots of plans for her—

The couch was empty and my stomach felt funny. Her dress was still on the floor though.

Bathroom? Nah. The door was open and the light off.

"Courtney?"

"In here."

I switched the cans so I had them both in one hand and used the other to brace myself on the doorframe to my bedroom. Her hair was messy from sex and her cheeks pink. She had the covers over her, but it didn't matter. The sight knocked me hard. It was only the woman I loved, naked in my bed.

No big deal.

"I like your bed," she said.

I stalked toward her. "Then, maybe stay a while."

Her voice was heavy with meaning, and she gave me the smile that made words fall out of my brain. "I think I will."

WHAT'S NEXT?

Wondering if there will be more Blindfold Club books? The answer is a definite YES! At least one, probably more. It's been brewing in the back of my mind since I began work on Torrid, and although I have other books scheduled before Book Six, I am hopeful I will publish it by the end of 2018.

ABOUT NIKKI

Nikki Sloane landed in graphic design after her careers as a waitress, a screenwriter, and a ballroom dance instructor fell through. For eight years she worked for a design firm in that extremely tall, black, and tiered building in Chicago which went through an unfortunate name change during her time there.

Now she lives in Kentucky, is married and has two sons. She is a two-time Romance Writers of America RITA© Finalist, also writes romantic suspense under the name Karyn Lawrence, and couldn't be any happier that people enjoy reading her sexy words.

Find her on the web: www.NikkiSloane.com

Contact her on Twitter: @AuthorNSloane

Send her an email: authornikkisloane@gmail.com

ALSO FROM NIKKI

DARK ROMANCE

SORDID

TORRID

SPORTS ROMANCE

THE RIVALRY

DRAZEN KINDLE WORLD

DESTROY

Made in the USA
Monee, IL
09 September 2024